# MENOETIUS

# MENOETIUS

by

**Jeff Lait**

2008
OneOff Enterprises

ISBN  978-0-9809011-1-5




OneOff Enterprises
Burlington, ON, Canada
e-mail: oneoffenterprises@gmail.com

*To my wonderful wife Caitilin*
*who always encourages me*
*to chase my dreams*

# Acknowledgements

I'd like to thank NaNoWriMo for providing the incentive to get this idea down in book form, my father for both joining me on that month of writing and working as the publisher, my mother for teaching what little I know of grammar, and most importantly my wife for listening to my ideas and pushing me to finish this book.

The first album by a band is said to represent the output of the band members entire life up to that point.  Likewise, this novel is not written from a *tabula resa*, but built on a lifetime of exploring other authors' worlds and ideas.  Hopefully the absence of any flying squirrels or references to Juptonium will assuage worries that this effort has fully mined my own past work.

# Chapter 1

*In which the scene is set for ensuing action.*

*W*eistling gazed out of the view port and sighed. The stars slowly moved from left to right, matching the slow spin of the station. Weistling looked down at the notebook he had in his hand and tried to focus his thoughts. The scratchy writing on the notebook would take a trained eye to decipher. In all likelihood, Weistling himself would not be able to read the notes. Still, the scrawled characters served their purpose in ordering scattered thoughts, and in triggering memories after the fact.

A faint chime alerted Weistling to the approach of another of the space station's inhabitants. Turning away from the wheeling stars, Weistling greeted the tall man who drifted into the observatory.

"Ah, good morning Adom. Are you here for me or for the black hole?"

Adom wasted no time with pleasantries. "Have you filled the FDR grant application yet?"

"That time of year again? Why do we have to bother? The Feds will never give us a grant. Black hole research hasn't been in style since before I was born."

"The application, I remind you, is mandatory. I sent you the forms ten days ago. Our internal review will be held in four days, and you are one of the few that have not yet responded." Adom turned and left the observatory.

"So much for real work..." Weistling muttered. Still, as frustrating as the bureaucracy could be, he could not complain. Black holes were passé in the physics community. His professors had tried to steer him away from the field, pointing out that Quantum and Casimir Effect studies had proven practical applications. Weistling was too much of a cynic to believe that was the true reason for the unpopularity of his chosen field of research. The real reason no one seriously studied black holes was about to drift by the view port in ten minutes.

Weistling flipped his notebook to a fresh page. A quick look through his unread mail showed that Adom had indeed sent him the application forms. Three days ago, not ten, but Weistling had to grudgingly admit that he was remiss for not having noticed them before. Copying the application forms onto the new page, he wondered if he would be the first to submit an FDR application. Adom's comment that Weistling was one of the few not to submit did not mean much on a space station with only three researchers.

Pulling up his previous year's application, Weistling began the extensive cut-and-paste job that was needed to fulfill his newest obligation. Comparing successive year's application forms was always instructive. Weistling learned that Black Hole Research was now categorized as a branch of Casimir Effect rather than Quantum. He wondered idly if the reclassification was seen as Quantum's loss or gain.

The incessant chime of his watch-alarm provided a welcome relief to the mindless filling of the FDR forms. Weistling looked back at the view port, his eyes watching the left hand side, eagerly awaiting the vista that had him isolated in this space station.

The dust halo was the first sign. A purple glow slowly slid into view. The purple glow deepened and reddened as more of the disk drifted into sight. The space station orbited in the plane of the disk, so the view was of the disk edge on. Weistling sometimes wished he could also enjoy the oblique angles, but seeing it from the side was no less breathtaking. All too soon, the slowly collapsing dust cloud that marked that-which-could-not-be-seen drifted out of the right hand side of the view port.

Menoetius, named by the first explorers after the Greek Titan, was what brought Weistling to this desolate part of the Confederacy. As humanity spread out from Earth on ships powered by the Casimir Effect, they discovered many strange and unusual things. No one had expected Menoetius, however. The Earth-massed black hole contradicted established doctrine. What was it doing in an otherwise unremarkable star system? How did a stable black hole with so little mass form?

Driven by these questions, and, as importantly, the opportunity to investigate a black hole close up, scientists flocked to the star system. Soon, the star itself took on Menoetius' name. A large and self-sufficient space station – the very one Weistling currently sat in – was built in orbit around Menoetius. In those days, grant money flowed freely to those studying black holes. Promises were made about new fields of physics being discovered, new sources of energy found, and alternative faster than light travel techniques revealed. And so the seeds of ruin were sown.

Menoetius was not to release his secrets so easily. After the initial excitement and extravagant theorization, all that was left was the hard work of data collection and experimentation. Physical constants were polished to another few decimal places. A few obscure, but unimportant, experiments were performed.

The fever passed almost as quickly as it had arisen. The young and brilliant physicists moved to more profitable fields. In their wake they left only a few facts resolved. Analysis of the rate of evaporation determined the age of the black hole. One hundred and fifty-three thousand years ago, an Earth-sized planet orbited this distant star. It was then converted, by apparently artificial means, into a black hole. Since no nearby systems showed any sign of intelligent life, it was concluded that whatever alien race that had accomplished this had disappeared into the hole, leaving a mute warning to any who would play too foolishly with the principles of physics.

Except, to this day, no one knew what those principles were.

When black hole research, despite having a live black hole to play with, failed to accomplish anything astounding, funding dried up. Fortunately for Weistling, a large multi-stellar had purchased a ninety-nine Earth-year maintenance contract on the space station. Having to maintain the space station as a matter of contract, they provided limited funding to any scholar willing to work so far from civilization.

Despite the funding being a tax write off, the multi-stellar still looked for ways to cut costs – hence the mandatory grant applications. Weistling looked back at his notebook, filled now with half completed forms rather than illegible notes, and sighed once more. Unlike the rest of the inhabitants of the space station, such as Kristina, a xenologist looking for traces of the lost alien race, or Stewart, a philosopher who was investigating the nature of Time by experiencing the influence of the gravitational effects of the black hole on light from distant stars, Weistling was here for the hole itself. He believed that Menoetius still had something to teach. He was not at all sure that it was useful (always a hindrance when writing a grant application), but he was sure that he wanted to know what it was.

# Chapter 2

*A woman with a gun and an exploding*
*spaceship.*

*R*hyta concentrated on her breathing. Each breath was taken with measured care, held for a count of two, and then slowly exhaled. While others would rely on the scout-suit, or on setting up noise damping fields, Rhyta believed in starting with the basics. If you weren't breathing, you were dead.

A quick glance through the thick bushes she had chosen for concealment revealed the worst. The small scout ship had held at least five men. All of them wore full combat suits. They had fanned out from the entrance of the ship, automatically spacing themselves to avoid providing a single target. That bespoke of training, which was worrying. One was studying a hand held sensor carefully. Judging by the colour of the sensor, Rhyta judged it to be a general purpose exploratory assessment device. That was good news – it suggested these people did not know the nature of this planet.

Rhyta knew the nature of this planet. There wasn't much on this planet in the nets. Such an embarrassing profusion of habitable planets had been found with humanity's expansion that frontier worlds, such as this one, barely rated a footnote. Unremarkable planets held a certain attraction for some people, however. Smugglers and fugitives both recognized the advantages that anonymity could provide. Rhyta had worked with both often enough to acquire her own personal database of likely hideaways.

Brestar's Star was a fine example of a fugitive planet. The sole city was honest enough, though it did possess a suspicious number of spacecraft for sale. And the city's revenues consisted in a large part of silence payments. Inbound spacecraft could, for a small fee, have their arrival to the other side of the world automatically erased from the satellite constellation before the city even downloaded the data. Even though she was on the right side of the law this time, Rhyta had availed herself of that service. To do otherwise would be to attract too much attention.

Turning back to her quarry, Rhyta cursed under her breath. A sixth man had left the spacecraft. This one, it seemed, was the commander. The combat suit's chameleon technology was thwarted by the presence of gold piping. Zooming in, she could pick out the insignia on the suit. Confederation – all the worse. If it came to a shooting match, she had better be twice as careful about not being recorded. Rhyta did not want to enjoy the life of a fugitive first hand just yet.

At least her information was good. She had not been certain about that. The hours spent hiking by foot through the untamed wilderness of Brestar's forest's had not been enjoyable – nor had the last three weeks camped by the supposed meeting place waiting for the ship to arrive. No chances could be taken, however. The presence of a landspeeder close to the secret meeting location would have scared her prey away as quickly as a painted sign.

To pass the time before the rendezvous, she checked over her emplacement. She had the high ground and a clear sight line on the clearing. She also had her ion-rifle setup on a tripod. A quick double check of the Casimir packs showed full charge. Not that they needed to be full. The ion-rifle's barrel was prone to overheating – she could only expect three shots from it before it would automatically shutdown for cooling. Well, it would shutdown if she had not already removed that safety. If she went past three, however, the fourth would likely warp the barrel, leaving the fifth ion blast with no clear path to go. The thought of that was not a pleasant one.

Rhyta sighted the clearing with the ion-rifle. The commander was looking at his watch. Rhyta knew there was still three minutes to the meeting, so suppressed the urge to do likewise. Instead, she breathed.

The air shook as a second ship screamed out of the sky. The five soldiers held their ground, but the commander took a step backwards in the face of the gale wind as the new ship's kinetic drive dumped energy into the atmosphere. The new ship was much smaller than the first. No doubt interstellar capable, but it likely only carried a crew of one. It took a certain type of person to fly such a ship. Not many people could handle the isolation between the stars.

It was a Falcon. A showy design with faux-aerodynamic metal wings swept back from a sharp, predatory, nose. The cockpit was that – a bubble of glassteel containing the sole occupant. The seal to the cockpit opened and the glass rose revealing the pilot. This pilot obviously knew the planet – he was not wearing a helmet. Knew the planet, and thought he knew the people already gathered in the clearing.

With practiced ease the pilot jumped out of the cockpit and onto the distressed meadow. Rhyta trained her parabolic microphone on the scene.

"Greetings Lieutenant Fracks!" spoke the newcomer. He strode briskly on the grass, showing no strain from the long time he must have spent cramped in his Falcon. He did not stand as tall as the commander, but he carried an authority that the lieutenant lacked. His short hair showed black against the blue-black of the lieutenant's combat suit. Rhyta had to acknowledge that with his dark eyes and space-pale skin he made an attractive sight.

"Trees have ears!" replied the lieutenant. "Sergeant, engage the damping field!"

One of the soldiers, no doubt the sergeant, returned to the ship. The lieutenant and the newcomer stood facing one another in silence. The newcomer gained some respect with Rhyta when she saw the humour in his eyes. He clearly realized the futility of noise damping fields if their previous precautions had been breached.

Shortly, the sergeant returned carrying a heavy box. No doubt he had hoped to not need to use it, as his expression was not one of joy. He ceremoniously flicked a large red switch on the side of the box. Rhyta's reception from the microphone went silent as the noise damper took effect. Rhyta sighed at the lieutenant's naivety and flipped her audio source from the parabolic microphone to the land line. At least she no longer had to feel foolish about burying an array of microphones under the suspected landing site.

"We are now secure, Jorge."

"As you wish, Lieutenant Fracks."

"This may seem like a game to you, but my Family will not look kindly on you if your mistakes delay our schedule. Have you got the penta-code?"

"Yes, I do. Have you got the payment? It wasn't easy prying that code out of the previous owner's hands. And, I don't think I need to remind you, lose the penta-code, and lose the data as surely as into a black hole."

"You need not fear my Family not upholding our end of our dealings, Jorge. Sergeant, retrieve the crate!"

The sergeant once again entered the ship. This time he returned with a sealed box, half a meter to a side, that he placed in front of Jorge. Jorge knelt down and opened the box. Silicon gleamed inside. Taking out a hand scanner, Jorge took out one of the silicon cubes at random and placed it in the scanner.

"Genuine Confederation CPU cores. Terahertz-certified. Very nice. We have a deal."

Jorge reached into his pocket and removed a small scrap of paper. A quick zoom verified he had folded it, preventing Rhyta from reading the penta-code through her scope. That would have been too easy, anyway.

"Paper, Jorge?" The lieutenant spat in disgust. Rhyta stifled a grin – the lieutenant had forgotten he still wore a combat helmet.

Lieutenant Fracks, eager to clean his visor, cracked and opened his helmet. He took it off to reveal a dark complexion with short red hair. Rhyta did not have to see the trademark goatee to know which Family Fracks was referring to. The S'dar dynasty was renowned for its distinctive dark skin and red hair. To be adopted into that family meant a voluntary genetic re-profiling to maintain that monopoly. Rumours existed of rogue geneticists that would provide the readjustment to people outside of the S'dar dynasty. Rhyta did not want to dwell on what the rumours said happened to impostors.

"Yes, paper. Be careful lest it blow away in the wind," remarked Jorge as he handed the small folded sheet over. Rhyta swore an oath under her breath. How had she thought she would get the code? She had hoped for two one-man fighters to have met. She'd have taken the chance with the ion-rifle then.

*Against seven men? This code wasn't worth that.* There was still hope, however. This Lieutenant Fracks was sloppy.

Jorge picked up the case of CPU cores and stored it in his ship's small hold. With a jaunty wave he jumped back into the cockpit and sealed the window around him. Meanwhile, the lieutenant had turned back to his ship and – by Earth! – was slowly unfolding the paper. Rhyta swung her scope onto the lieutenant and concentrated on breathing while waiting for a clean shot.

The lieutenant shook his head over the inscription and quickly refolded the paper. Not before Rhyta had read and recorded the contents, however:

```
QS6UT-B70CH-9BRSM-86SD5-MA3LE+EAFRB-DN9JQ-
PK6DK
```

*Bingo!* Rhyta watched in amusement as the lieutenant carefully put the paper into his pocket. *How did the S'dar dynasty find such an inept tool?* Returning her gaze to the full scene, she saw Jorge's Falcon slowly rise off the meadow shrouded by a haze of frost. Lieutenant Fracks also watched the Falcon's departure with a decidedly predatory grin. Rhyta did not like that look.

Sure enough, the Falcon had barely reached five hundred meters when a large gout of flame erupted from its underside. A thundering boom accompanied the pyrotechnics and the Falcon lurched suddenly to the left and began to plummet to the ground. Rhyta glanced at her ion rifle to see the EMP fuses had triggered. *That explains the loss of control – that close the electromagnetic pulse likely knocked out his whole flight system.* The lieutenant grinned at the burst of fire. As the hapless Falcon disappeared beneath the trees, he turned back to his ship's airlock. His squad of soldiers followed, the noise damper, now disabled by the electromagnetic pulse, carried by the sergeant. Rhyta's gaze followed the Falcon down, projecting its likely crash location. All too close to her hidden base. This job had just got another complication.

# Chapter 3

*In which we are lectured on some of the
fundamental limitations placed on Life by the
Universe, delivered by an esteemed professor
who shall be introduced properly much later.*

*T*he laws of the universe are the only limit on the diver-
sity of Life. Unfortunately, careful analysis shows that
rather than creating a set of prohibitions, the nature of the
Universe is better expressed by saying "Anything not explicitly
permitted is forbidden."

The most obvious example of this is in the realm of thermodynamics. While one can reduce entropy in one location, it is
always at the expense of greater entropy in the surrounding
system. The Universe, observation tells us, is a closed system.
As such, all of Life must fit within whatever entropy is available
to it.

Less obvious are the tight rules that govern the rise of new
civilizations. Statistic analysis of Life-compatible planets shows
how rare the individualistic intelligence required to create technology is. While plant and animal analogues are quite common,
we rarely find any entity that questions if there is anything
beyond eat-or-be-eaten. When these do occur, one would expect
there to at least be a wide variety of potential civilizations.
Again, there is not. Consider a new alien race that has just
begun to acquire technology. We could envision that there is a
free choice as to how quickly it would develop the technology.

It could slowly adapt over a hundred thousand years, or quickly discover and change within a few hundred.

Indeed, we have found vanished examples of both types of civilizations. The chances of us meeting one is highly unlikely, however. If the civilization advances too quickly, they will destroy themselves before we can make contact. If they advance too slowly, the twists and turns of their own planets ecology are bound to usurp them before they develop sufficient electro-magnetic transmissions for us to detect them.

Careful study of group-dynamics simulations shows a very small area where these two factors balance out. If a civilization would take much less than ten thousand years to go from radio transmissions to space travel, its resource consumption will destroy it within a hundred years. If a civilization would take much longer than ten thousand years, it would never develop radio transmission before the next ice age-like event wiped it out.

These two opposing tipping points constrain intelligent, space faring, civilizations to a very small wedge of the potentials of Life. And thus, again, the immutable laws of the Universe seek to constrain our actions.

One useful result from this study has been the optimization of the search for intelligent life. By monitoring all systems in a five thousand light year radius on a five thousand year interval, one can, with great probability, respond to all new civilizations before they have achieved spaceflight.

# Chapter 4

*In which we watch Jorge plummet from the sky
to certain death.*

*J*orge waited until the cockpit had closed before shaking his head. Acquiring the code had been no small job and had been a good test of his skills. The manner of delivery was anti-climatic.

*Does the S'dar dynasty think I am not worth better than that flunky?*

Jorge jabbed the launch button with his thumb and quelled these black thoughts. At least he had the CPU cores. Powerful processors fetched a good markup on the frontier worlds – especially cores with the Confederation manufacturing seal.

A chill fell over the cockpit as the Falcon's kinetic drive kicked in, converting ambient heat into vertical momentum. Jorge barely noticed this, being accustomed to even greater bone-chilling maneuvers in the depths of space. He glanced at the altimeter readout and watched it scroll upwards, leaving this forsaken fugitive world behind. Jorge had some bad memories of Brestar's Star. A deal gone wrong had seen him abandoned here, forced to work to earn sufficient passage to escape off world to where the price for ships was more reasonable. If there was one thing Jorge hated, it was hard work.

The world flashed white.

A sharp concussion jolted Jorge against his harness straps.

The white faded into a grey scale, and the grey slowly gave way to colour, but what it revealed didn't please Jorge much more than the white had. His instrument panel was dead. His view port showed the landscape rushing to greet him once more.

Jorge's reactions were not those of his conscious mind. He was still watching the white resolve into grey when his hand flipped open a safety latch to expose a red switch underneath. When his finger flicked the switch he felt another sharp bite of cold. His subconscious noted that the kinetic drive was still on-line so let the hardened crash computer complete its simple programming.

In a state of shock, Jorge's conscious mind watched numbly as the trees of the forest rushed toward him. Jorge braced for impact. He knew as he did so that it was futile – at this speed he would be flattened against the glassteel – presuming the armoured surface would survive the impact.

As the Falcon fell below the leading trees, the trees burst into flame. At the same time, the Falcon slowed to a stop – the kinetic drive having dumped its motion into the ensuing inferno. Jorge allowed himself to laugh out loud as his ship made a perfect landing in the middle of conflagration.

*Looks like I was smarter than I gave myself credit for.* What Jorge had forgotten in the shock of the treachery was his paranoid preparations. He had very carefully programmed the backup guidance system – a system hardened against just this sort of EMP attack. The best defense in the face of this sort of treachery was to let the other side believe they had won. The crash computer's program was to let the ship fall uncontrolled until the last second, during which an emergency dump of the acquired momentum would produce a satisfactory fireball. A good adversary would investigate to verify that the ship was destroyed. Jorge, however, felt he could rely on Lieutenant Flacks to not be a good adversary.

Jorge waited patiently for fifteen minutes as the forest fire petered out. The flash heating had only cooked off the closest trees; the season was still too wet for the fire to spread.

When the fire was reduced to embers and glowing smoke, and the external thermometer showed the temperature a bearable thirty centigrade, Jorge again opened the cockpit. His boots crackled as they landed on still-hot carbonized wood.

"Let's see what they did to you, baby," spoke Jorge as he inspected the underbelly of his ship.

As expected from the concussion, the door to the cargo hold that had held the CPU cores had been blown out. The inside was blackened but the hull metal had not bent in response to the force. The explosion had been successfully diverted out the weakest point – the external hatch – thereby not damaging the ship proper. A bit of cleaning and a new hatch cover and the cargo hold would be as good as new; accounting for the potential of explosive cargo was standard operating procedure in Jorge's circles.

With the attention he gave his own ship, it was not surprising that it took Jorge a few hours to realize that, not more than fifty meters away, rested another Falcon hiding under the forest canopy.

# Chapter 5

*In which Weistling discusses the nature of the
vanished race with Kristina and Stewart
provides some valuable insights.*

*W*eistling sat in his self-styled control center and
watched the black hole spin.

He sat loosely strapped into a large chair. His notebook lay
within easy reach and opened to a blank page. Two large
screens – a meter across each – were set up showing data from
the black hole. One screen showed the data in the raw – a series
of scrolling text windows and slowly advancing graphs detailing
the feedback from the observational satellites. The other screen
showed a composite video image rendered in beautiful false
colour.

The incoming data came from a constellation of thirty
satellites orbiting the black hole at sufficient distance to avoid
disintegrating in the dust cloud. Because transmitting data close
to the black hole was an exercise in futility, the far satellites sent
their data to the neighbouring satellites rather than directly back
to the space station. The resulting series of speed-of-light delays
resulted in a five second time difference between the far
satellites and the close satellites. One of the first things
Weistling did with the data stream was to buffer the data and
resynchronize it to provide simultaneous data feeds from all of
the satellites. The previous physicist had been a more devoted
student of Einstein and had refused such resynchronizations for
two excellent reasons. First, there is no such thing as simul-

taneity. What common sense calls "simultaneous" is a highly observer-dependent phenomenon. Second, even so far as one could construct an ad hoc idea of "simultaneous" when synchronizing a communication network around a normal planet, the vicinity of a black hole further complicated the issue and once supposed constants, like the rate of passage of time, could not be relied upon. One advantage of being the sole token physicist on a corporate death-watch, however, was the ability to write one's own rules. So, Weistling had carefully calibrated the data feeds until he had this: his control center. The most useful advantage of the built-in tape delay was the ability to composite the different video footages to produce the amazing image on his left monitor. By splicing the feeds from different satellites, he could freely fly about and fly into the black hole in what felt like real time.

A faint chime alerted Weistling that he had company in his sanctum. He stayed staring at the slowly spinning black hole, partly hypnotized by it and the continuous stream of data on his right screen. A soft female voice broke the spell.

"Good afternoon, Weistling. See any artifacts in that dust cloud yet?" inquired Kristina, the resident xenologist, in a light manner.

"There was a suicide note from the lost alien-race that went by earlier, but I didn't bother to record it. I hope that wasn't of interest?" replied Weistling in a teasing tone.

"Of no import. As you know, I don't favour the suicide-hypothesis. If you had recorded it, I'd have no choice but see that you deleted it."

"That is the official conclusion in textbooks, however. An alien race achieved much power, but then, overtaken by a nihilistic death-cult, turned their home world into a black hole.

Said cult, being conveniently nihilistic, then went to extreme lengths to ensure no trace remained. Hence there are no artifacts, and no reason for you to be here."

Kristina rose to the bait at once.

"As I recall, the official conclusion in the textbooks also states that Menoetius, while an intriguing example of a small-scale black hole, merely verifies long held theories about relativity, black holes, etc, and has nothing new to offer. The special knowledge of physics that the lost alien race used to create the black hole vanished down the event horizon hundreds of thousands of years ago. Hence there is no physics to be done here, and no reason for you to be here."

"A good point," conceded Weistling in a conciliatory tone. "All of us here are misfits of some sort or other. It stands to reason that those who accept the current dogma would not want to bother coming to the tail-end of the Universe to verify what they already know. That sad task is left to those who seek to prove the opposite."

"What is it you expect to prove, Weistling? You seem to spend all of your time just developing more elaborate ways of monitoring. I can't recall you engaging in any active experiments."

Weistling paused, thinking on his answer. He wasn't much given to soul searching, much preferring to lose himself in mathematics than philosophy. At least with math you had a chance of proving yourself right.

"I'm not performing experiments largely because, historically, that has meant throwing different objects at the hole just to see what happens. I want to perform an experiment when I know what the answer will be. Menoetius is a not an natural creation, but an artifact of some intelligent creature. As such, it must be a tool. I want to find what, and how, it is used. I'm pretty sure a black hole wasn't created just to provide a convenient way to dispose of garbage."

"Careful, Weistling, you are drifting into my specialty! To play the devil's advocate, why are you convinced it is a tool? Humans build many things other than tools. We build art, for example. We also build many things we don't intend to. Earth still has no shortage of unlivable areas, places so polluted as to be deadly to all life."

Weistling snorted at these possibilities. "I don't think you think that way, or you wouldn't be here. Unlike you, however, I don't need to justify why I think it is a tool. I just have to justify there is some chance of applying it."

"So, to change the subject, how's your grant application going?"

"Submitted it yesterday," replied Weistling.

"Always the first, eh? I like to let Adom stew for a bit. Helps him feel important if he can have something to enforce. I'm trying a different tack this year. I hold with your tool theory – Menoetius is artificial and intentional and serves some purpose. The question for us Xenologists is why there is no trace of whoever did it. I've spent the last five years combing this system from end to end. It had all been combed before, but we all hold our hope of finding that lost suicide-note. This year I'll be advancing the theory that the absence shows that the Alien Race wasn't native to this star system at all. They came from outside, setup the black hole, and left. If the aliens had developed locally, they would have surely launched some artifacts into space prior to collapsing the hole. Even if they turned nihilistic, it would be prohibitively difficult to catch up to and track down all of those artifacts. Earth still has the Voyager satellites slowly meandering into interstellar space, for example. The inability for our own, much more advanced, science to determine how to create our own black holes – even with one available as evidence that it is possible – provides ample proof that any race that did develop the technology would have also developed spaceflight."

"So, if no traces remain, what would keep you here?" asked Weistling, wondering if Kristina had escaped the gravitational tug of Menoetius.

"Traces will remain. They had to enter and leave this star system. As such, there will be contamination in the interstellar gases. I've read some papers on spaceship tracking technologies. Kinetic drives, unless properly shielded, leave tell-tale wakes that could theoretically be preserved for millions of years. Some of the newly developed detection protocols could be applied to our sensors and a sweep could be performed looking for such ancient wakes."

"Ah, the Robinson Crusoe Hypothesis, no? Proposed by Dr. Findley fifty years ago, if I recall correctly," interjected a new voice in the room. Stewart, the resident philosopher, had entered sometime during the conversation. He was a large, heavyset man who worked hard to maintain a disheveled appearance at all times. This time was not an exception – his anachronistic tweed jacket actually managed to look rumpled.

Kristina's face froze at the comment. Weistling almost sighed – had she hoped that her thoughts were actually original? In a field that had been so thoroughly studied that most arguments had moved well into the metaphysical? Stewart, as usual unaware of the calamitous effect that he could have, continued his contribution to the discussion.

"I came across a reference to it when preparing my grant application this morning. I was dredging through cross references on time and stumbled across it quite by accident. It was published in a very minor journal and the only comments were highly negative. Still, a fascinating hypothesis! Dr. Findley believed that Menoetius was created, as Kristina has been describing, by visiting aliens rather than by locals. Dr. Findley advanced the supposition that the aliens had become stranded in this star system. Without a functioning FTL system they had no way of returning home on their own. They were able to signal for help, but the inevitable speed of light delays would mean such a signal would take tens of thousands of years to be received. The solution was simple – construct a black hole, dive into it to a sufficient depth that the gravitational effect slowed time substantially, and await rescue."

"Dr. Findley was clearly no physicist," spat Weistling. "To go deep enough into an Earth-massed black hole to experience non-negligible gravitational slowing would expose you to tidal stresses that would exceed the theoretical bounds of the strongest materials! Besides, that fairy tale suggests the aliens had sufficient technology to build a black hole, but not enough to repair their FTL drive? Kinetic drives are ridiculously simple devices – I wouldn't be surprised if there is a home FTL drive building kit available for school children."

"Yes, that is pretty much what the comments on Dr. Findley's paper were," replied Stewart, unfazed by Weistling's vehemence. "If you would like the reference, Kristina, I can forward it to you?"

"Yes, please, Stewart. I'm sure it would make an interesting footnote," replied Kristina, slightly muffled through her gritted teeth.

Jeff Lait

When Stewart had left the room with as little ceremony as he had arrived, Kristina vented her emotions:

"To Venus with that scoundrel. Could he not let me have at least a day to think I had something worthwhile? Well, I need not bother you with this, then!" Kristina's notebook bounced off the wall. Weistling carefully reached up and caught it on the return bounce. He glanced at the top page – the scanning procedures for detecting starship wakes. His mind was instantly captured by the procedures outlined. It required careful synchronization across multiple observational platforms, careful compilation and analysis of the resulting data streams, and provided some innovative algorithms to post-process the result. The procedures covered all possibilities: ships with kinetic drives, ships with ion drives, even ships with chemical rocket drives. Weistling wondered why they bothered with that test – how could a rocket ship carry enough fuel for an interstellar transit? The answer suddenly dawned on him.

"This scanning protocol isn't used to track *interstellar* transit, is it?"

Kristina, her rage expended in throwing her notebook, looked abashed.

"No, it isn't. It is designed for finding the lairs of pirates. Straight from a Confederation Naval Handbook. The adaptation to tracking interstellar wakes is straight forward, however. On one of the other pages details the protocols which cover that."

"Despite Stewart's comments, Findley couldn't have had any evidence. These techniques weren't around fifty years ago. The foolishness of Findley's hypothesis no doubt meant no one attempted any good scanning of the interstellar dust outside of Menoetius' heliosphere. With this, you could find the first piece of concrete evidence."

"Thank you... Could you please set up the scanning system then?"

"I thought you would never ask," replied Weistling.

# Chapter 6

*In which Rhyta and Jorge meet face to face and arrange a temporary truce.*

**R**hyta gazed down the sights of her ion rifle and cursed. It had taken a good four hours of hiking through the dense underbrush of the Brestar's forest to reach her concealed Falcon spacecraft. Despite Jorge's ship having crashed in the direction of her base camp, she had still been happy. Her mission accomplished, she was eager to get off this world and deliver the penta-code to the AIs who had commissioned her.

As she grew closer to her ship, her mood started to sour. The smoke cloud from the crashed spaceship was growing closer. The trees it came from looked suspiciously familiar. Safety outweighing speed, she slowed down and swung to the north, approaching her ship from the far side. If Jorge had survived, he just might have set up an ambush expecting a straight line approach.

Eventually she worked herself to a concealed hill overlooking her disguised spaceship. With the zoom of the ion-rifle she could clearly make out the worst of her fears. About sixty meters away from her ship was a clearing burned out of the surrounding forest. In the middle of it was Jorge's Falcon, resting apparently undamaged on its landing gear. If it wasn't for the charred forest around it, she would not have believed it to be the ship she saw fall helpless out of the sky. Clearly Jorge was a more skilled operator than Lieutenant Fracks.

That alone would be enough to put a damper on her spirits. Unfortunately, things only got worse. Leaning against *her* Falcon was Jorge. He wore his combat armour but he still did not wear a helmet. His expression was relaxed, as if they had made an arrangement to meet there.

Rhyta considered her options carefully. A shot with her ion-rifle could end this problem right here. Rhyta had no quarrel with Jorge, however. His lack of helmet also convinced her to not start shooting first. Jorge clearly was interested in some form of parley. Perhaps his ship was more damaged than it seemed. With the power of the EMP blast, it was possible that the computer system had been wiped out. That seemed unlikely, however, as if the computer system had been off-lined, his ship should be lying in a crater, not on its landing gear.

The other option was to avoid the engagement entirely. As per standard procedure, she could set-up a one-time-pad encrypted channel to her ship. She could retreat to another clearing, request the ship to meet her there, and then make her escape. Unfortunately, if Jorge's ship was operational, it would be trivial to follow her. He also may have identified her ship, so could conceivably inform the S'dar that their penta-code might be compromised. That wouldn't reduce the value of the penta-code to Rhyta's clients – there being no effective way to erase information – but the S'dar dynasty may decide to take vengeance on the one who stole their codes. That is another complication Rhyta did not want to have.

Rhyta sighed. *It looks like we'll have to do this the old fashioned way – diplomacy.*

"Hullo, stranger!" Rhyta called out. She stepped out of concealment with her ion rifle casually slung over her shoulder. More than a few people had made the mistake of thinking it would take her a long time to get a clean shot from that stance. No one had lived to make the mistake twice.

Rhyta was pleased to see Jorge start at the sound of her voice. He had clearly expected her arrival from the direction of the meeting place.

Jorge gave her a careful appraisal before answering. The time his eyes spent on her ion rifle showed that he wasn't one to be so foolish as to underestimate how long it would take her to fire. He wisely kept his hands in sight as he replied slowly. His voice was level, showing a composure belied by his earlier jump.

"Greetings. My apologies for trespassing on your space here. With the skill you took in hiding it, however, I hope you realize it was not of my choice. I'm not sure I could have found your ship if I had been looking for it. It seems the best way to locate a lost needle is to jump into the haystack," joked Jorge, gesturing to his own ship.

Rhyta did not grin at the joke, instead replying coldly, "Flattery will get you no where. What is your name and purpose here?"

Jorge laughed again. "So we will play that game, eh? I'm pretty sure you know my name, but I will entertain you. I'm Jorge, and I came to the wrong-side of Brestar to conduct the sort of business best done on the wrong-side of Brestar."

"I fear your fame is not so great as you may believe, Jorge, for I do not know you. I did see your ship fall out of the sky trailing flames, however. I must give credit that it is still in one piece rather than a crater."

"Thank you. That is part of my problem, however. My business associate decided to not play very nicely. The payment for my hard work consisted of an explosive charge and an EMP blast powerful enough to make one forget one's own name. Fortunately, I had a hardened backup flight computer for just such a purpose. Unfortunately, it's not that powerful a computer. I could fly out of here on it, but I'd be limping at best. I'd rather not check in at the local starport for repairs.

"Just when I was wondering how I was going to find the code for a Falcon Flight Computer on the wrong side of Brestar, I noticed your ship. I ask you, as a fellow traveler, for the courtesy of a bootstrap for my ship."

"You mean to tell me..." asked Rhyta, dumbfounded, "that you had a backup computer pre-programmed to simulate a fiery crash, but hadn't bothered to make a backup of your flight computer's code to restore from? That'd fit on a data cube with plenty of room to spare!"

Jorge had the decency to look abashed at the accusation.

"I do have a backup. Unfortunately, it is... old. As a fellow Falcon flier, I'm sure you know there have been many important patches since then. And, as for my emergency escape plan – the original plan involved self-destructing *Freia*, my ship, to make just the crater you would expect. When I saw my adversary fly off to space without having bothered to sweep the crash site, I grew soft-hearted. Also, I'd rather fly out of here than hike around this planet looking for passage."

"It's a poor pilot that would abandon his ship," commented Rhyta, unimpressed with Jorge's self-destruction plan. She had locked out *Melfar*'s self-destruction codes because she did not even want that option to be available to her.

"Well, what do you say? I'd offer payment, but my stock of hard tradeables went "poof" with the explosion. And I suspect you don't want an IOU, as you don't want me to be able to identify you to those I met back in that clearing." Jorge jerked a thumb back in the direction that the meeting had took place.

"Business on Brestar stays on Brestar," spoke Rhyta firmly. "I don't want anything to do with the sort of business that gets your friends planting EMPs on your ship. However, in this universe, the best prepared can find themselves in a hitch. Or, in your case, the ill-prepared, but I hope karma doesn't pay too much attention to the difference. I'll build you a Falcon startup sequence. On two conditions. First, this meeting never took place. While my purposes here are legal..." – Jorge snorted as she made that claim – "... it seems clear that your purposes are more shadowy. And I do not want to be mixed up with them. Second, you must reinstall your flight system when you next reach a port. I'll be stripping my flight system of my personal modifications, but I may leave some. Again, I don't want to be fingerprinted by some stale data on *Freia*'s systems."

"Those conditions sound quite sensible," agreed Jorge. "You have my word, for what little it is worth. If you have any doubts, remember I was just betrayed by those at my last meeting. Even if there was a third party spying on the procedure, I'm of no mood to alert my ex-business partners about it now. It is best for me if they continue to think me dead."

"Very well. It will take me a while to build a new image for you. Wait in your ship and I will tight-beam you the new image. When you have tested it, I want you to fly out and go interstellar as quickly as you can manage. I'd like my privacy when I make my own way off this world."

"Thank you very much. I hope karma does repay your kindness some day." With a short bow, Jorge turned back to his ship.

# Chapter 7

*In which a scan is made of Menoetius's*
*heliosphere and the remains of spaceship wakes*
*are found.*

Kristina walked into Weistling's control room to find him sitting back with a wide smile on his face.

"I got your call, Weistling. Did you figure out the scanning procedures I gave you?" Kristina asked. She felt the question could be classified as rhetorical – Weistling's exuberance suggested that he had a new toy and was eager to show it off.

"It was difficult. To detect the variance caused by a kinetic drive requires a sweep of a volume of over ten light minutes. The differences need to be synchronized within hundreds of a millisecond. This requires an accuracy of position and velocity that would seem to be limited by Heisenberg!" Weistling was standing by the end of this speech. His tone was that of a great prophet making a momentous declaration. Kristina could not resist bringing him back down.

"I am no student of physics, Weistling, but that does not mean I'm unaware of Heisenberg's Uncertainty Principle. And the order of magnitude involved. Which you are nowhere near."

"Please, I have done the impossible! Let me have my hyperbole! You have arrived at a fortuitous moment. Everything is in place. With a press of a button, your scan will commence!"

Kristina looked doubtfully in the direction that Weistling had gestured. On the left monitor was a single large button labeled "Start Scan". It slowly pulsed red. On the right monitor was a slowly rotating image of the heliosphere of Menoetius rendered in exquisite detail. *I would give this job to someone with a sense of the theatric*, sighed Kristina.

"How far is it to the heliosphere, Weistling?"

"Er... Fourteen light-hours to the close side?"

"So, I press the button to commence the scan. The signal is then sent off to the probes placed out there. Fourteen hours to get the start command. Then fourteen hours to start receiving data. At least I hope you haven't requisitioned an FTL capable probe just for the purpose of shuttling data!"

Weistling grinned mischievously. Too late, Kristina realized she had fallen into his trap. "You give me no credit, Kristina. I would not be so cruel as devise a system that requires you to wait a full day to get results. When you press that button, the map on the right will start to fill in with data. As sections of the heliosphere are scanned, they will be coloured in with a green tint. Slowly the entire map will turn green. That process will, of course, take a long time – I'm estimating a month to do a full scan. If the system detects any trails, they will be drawn into the map as blue rays leading off into interstellar space, pointing out which direction the ship had gone."

"Instantly? How?"

"A magician never reveals his secrets!" was Weistling's proud reply.

"You couldn't have done this by predicting when I'll press the button and timing the scan to start at that moment. You couldn't know how long it would take me to respond to your message. Or how long we'd spend bantering before I took the plunge."

Kristina's thoughts went back to what she normally saw on the right hand monitor – Menoetius slowly rotating. Weistling had been very proud of that image. "No... You wouldn't..."

Weistling just grinned.

"The probes are already running, aren't they? You have already received data and are just buffering it locally, pressing that button will only start the processing!"

The change in Weistling's face showed that Kristina had figured out his planned method. "Until the data is observed, it doesn't exist. Thus, it is not until the button is pressed that the probes will have been known to have started working, and hence the scan to have started. You don't complain about the two hundred millisecond buffer between your eyes and your conscious, I don't see why you claim a mere ten hour data delay here is any less real time."

"You've been collecting data for ten hours!" shouted Kristina. "Hit that button, NOW!"

Obligingly, Weistling hit the large glowing button with the palm of his hand. It was replaced by a stream of numbers showing data being processed. Kristina watched it, hypnotized by the flow of information, barely catching a number here or there that made any sense. After two minutes a scan block was completed and a section of the heliosphere blinked as it changed from black tint to green tint.

"Ah, first sweep complete!" exclaimed Weistling, happy to see his toy in action.

"Complete ten hours ago." commented Kristina sourly.

"Now, now. You already lectured me about the fourteen hour speed of light delay. It was actually completed twenty-four hours ago. But simultaneous is in the eyes of the observer. And for us, the observers, it just completed."

They both sat back and watched the heliosphere change colour.

"You said the scan would take a month?"

"Yes. Little reason to expect anything in the first half hour."

"True, but still one cannot help but hope."

"I know. I counted on that."

Kristina wondered at Weistling's knowing grin. Her thoughts were cut short by a sudden change on the heliosphere display. A red line of text scrolled by the text screen. A dark blue ray appeared in the heliosphere, stabbing out from the most recent scanned sector.

"What! A blue ray? A flight path?" shouted Kristina, shocked and overjoyed.

"Excellent! It works!" echoed Weistling.

"So much for probability! I can't believe we struck pay dirt so quickly! Can you do a reverse-analysis and figure out where that ship came from?"

"Trevak's Star," replied Weistling immediately, without so much as a glance at his notebook. He had his knowing grin back on.

"Trevak's Star? But that is explored space. Indeed, isn't that where we get our supply shipments from....? Oh."

The first blue ray had been joined by a thick cluster of rays in the same sector. All pointing in the same direction.

"A scanning system to detect the alien's drive wakes would also detect our wakes. Thus, I started the search in the common approach route so we could verify we could at least pick up our own drive trails. Well, a bit outside of the approach route. Had to give time to build the suspense."

"You...." Epithets failed Kristina. She decided to divert the discussion rather than focus on how well she had been played. "With all of our own mucking about in the heliosphere, how will we detect the alien wakes? What if they did come from Trevak's star?"

"Fortunately, the station's memory has a list of all inbound ship traffic. They installed a pretty good traffic control system for what would eventually be a deserted star system. I've cross referenced with that list so all known ship wake's are drawn in the dark blue. If we get anything new, we'll get a flashing red wake."

"How nice of you to have explained that from the beginning."

"You are very welcome."

Weistling and Kristina both settled back, watching the heliosphere slowly turn green, punctured occasionally by another blue-ray of an off-course spacecraft.

# Chapter 8

*In which the unnamed lecturer provides important information about the nature of Intelligence.*

*I*n previous lectures, we examined the narrow window of potential civilizations created by the laws of the universe. These same laws constrain almost every other aspect of our existence.

Consider the question of the maximum potential intelligence in an alien species. We have seen that the rate of an alien civilization's development is constrained by the rate of their resource usage. If the civilization progresses too quickly, it will exhaust its home world's resources before making the long jump to interstellar space. This, however, does not seem to place any limits on the maximum development of the civilization. We could imagine the intelligence of the alien race continuing to develop at a slower, sustainable pace. Even without resorting to questionable exponential increase, even with assuming that intelligence increase is merely linear, we would expect the alien race's intelligence to be vastly superior to our own after, say, a million years.

This, we have seen from direct observation, has not been the case. While the knowledge base, and the toolset, of the civilization increase considerably, the maximum cognitive ability plateaus even before spaceflight is discovered!

To understand this paradox, it is important to revisit what it is we mean by intelligence. Intelligence isn't mere computational power. Intelligence implies more than rote execution of prewritten instructions. Intelligence implies a certain chaos that lets it stand away from the stream of code and edit itself. This self-referential capability is both what defines and constrains intelligence.

An analogy I like to present is that of a dripping water faucet. With the faucet only slightly open, a slow and steady drip falls out. By timing the rate of the water drops one can predict the next drop accurately. The amount of state you need to describe the system and reproduce it is very little: the time of the last drop and the time between drops. This is your traditional digital computer. Each tick of the clock advances all of the components in an orderly and proscribed fashion. If the faucet is opened a little bit more, something interesting occurs. The drops become erratic. Chaos has entered the system. The state information has grown: small changes in initial conditions determine large differences in the end result. This is where intelligence can be found. What happens if we try to increase the flow still further? For a while, the flow becomes more complicated: braided threads of water vie to be the principle route. But then another state transition occurs: the flow becomes smooth and laminar. This high-speed flow is once more amenable to analysis. The complex state-information embodied in the intermittent flow is lost. A simple equation of velocity and pressure fully describes the system.

Keep this analogy in your minds and consider a simple calcu-lating machine as equivalent to simple minds. As more neurons are added, more interconnections created, and the speed of processing is increased, the systems state becomes entangled with itself. At a certain point, self awareness begins and the entity can start to effectively edit itself. Most young societies conclude that further intelligence can be created by just increasing the number of processing units. Or increasing the clock frequency. This does work, up to a point. Eventually, however, the system changes state again. The complete system becomes too complex to model itself. Event propagation within the mind can no longer affect the whole mind. The consciousness becomes laminar, boring, and ineffective. Like the fully opened tap.

Psychologists have often noticed this among the exceptional individuals of any given species. Often, the instability of the geniuses is attributed to them lying on the far end of the bell-curve. However, it is also a result of their treading too close to the other end of chaos: noise. Chaos taken too far becomes mere noise. Noise, like the molecules in the fast-moving trap, is trivial to model with statistical methods. Our journey from the simple deterministic system thus ends up back with a simple deterministic system due to the Law of Large Numbers.

We can thus discount the specter of a Machine Intelligence that will supplant organics through superior intellect. Any artificial intelligence system is inhibited by the same fundamental laws of statistics as a natural organic system. Since the organic system has already been perfected by the time the alien race can create an artificial intelligence, the use of machines to do thinking is of little use. It is much cheaper and efficient to use the ready-made organic creatures.

Another common misconception about machine intelligence is that it would allow for entities to back themselves up. The idea runs that, since the intelligence is digital, one can exactly record its state at a certain time. This recorded state could then be restored if anything happens to the original copy. Or it could be duplicated to multiply the entity.

Neither of these things are possible for the same reason they are not possible in the organic case. The machine intelligence, like the organic intelligence, is walking a tight rope of chaos between two types of order. The order of trivial simplicity on one hand, and the order of white noise on the other hand. Being derived from chaos, the creature is highly sensitive to its original state. Indeed, the more powerful the intellect, the more entwined its state is. There is thus no simple clock to stop to let one read off the current state. Any attempt to read the state must be done while the mind is still in flux. Rather than capturing an image at a single point, one will capture an image which spans a considerable length of time. If one tries to rebuild the system using this scan, the resulting confusion will tip the intelligence into the abyss of chaos. If one tries to slow the system down so it is possible to perform an effectively instantaneous scan, it will plummet into the abyss of simplicity. In neither case can the mind be restored.

The final common myth is that of an Omega Point. Foolish civilizations – often those that will burn out before contact – watch their increasing processing power and draw exponential predictions. They come to illogical conclusions, the most common of which is that at some point the computing power would be sufficient to model all existing living creatures. They call this the Omega Point and reason that the resulting computer could be used to resurrect all that came before it. It is a sign of a confused mind that would accept these sort of conclusions rather than realizing that such a conclusion is actually proof that the exponential model must be untenable.

With these facts, we can see why the stalemate has existed so long between the machines and us. We both live in the same galaxy, governed by the same immutable principles of physics.

What isn't clear is why there exists a war at all. Why is it that friendship between organic and machine intelligence is not an option?

# Chapter 9

*In which Rhyta watches Jorge leave Brestar.*

**R**hyta waited until Jorge had entered his ship before entering her own. As the cockpit canopy closed over her, she called out: "Melfar? You catch that exchange?"

Silence greeted her question.

"Sheesh! Sometimes I think I really am flying solo!" Rhyta stabbed a violet button on her console marked *Wake Up*.

A synthetic voice spoke: "You are back early, Rhyta! Sorry for not sensing your approach. I was caught up analyzing some deep and complicated mathematical structures."

"I might be more inclined to believe you, Melfar, if you ever showed any talent at math. I'd place my bets that you were playing that new game you downloaded at the last system. Why don't you stop trying to justify your failure to maintain even the slightest of watches, and take a look out the external sensors?"

"Oh... My... Where did that ship come from?"

"Like most spaceships, from the sky. As you'd have known if you had put the stupidest of watchdog programs on the external sensors. I can't believe it. A bloody spaceship crashes next to you and you don't even look up from your game!"

"How're we supposed to get a baseline computer system for him?" asked Melfar, eager to distract Rhyta from the tirade she was building up to.

"Well, at least you can still use rewind effectively. We're going to get a baseline system by going over our existing system

41

and removing all of the bonus stuff that we've integrated over the last few years."

"But! That's millions of lines of code!"

"Most of which we have never touched, I'll remind you. And under revision control. We just roll back to the base state, and then apply any forward patches that weren't written by us. Simple enough?"

"Crazy grunt work, if you ask me. Why don't we just leave him here? Someone who lets their ship be EMPed deserves to take the long walk to civilization."

"One good turn deserves another, Melfar. We have the code. We can afford to be generous. Next time it might be us needing someone's grunt work. Now, let's get to work."

Rhyta plugged herself into the ship's computer system. The view out the cockpit was replaced by several large text consoles. One advantage of write-only-once memory systems was that you did not have to worry about losing old versions of your code. However, just having an earlier copy would not suffice. As Jorge had pointed out, several important patches had come down the pipe since the Falcon was commissioned. Some of those had serious security concerns – some flight parameters were randomized with insufficient entropy, allowing an attacker to predict the standard evasive patterns. Normally a pilot would have their own set of evasive patterns programmed, but Jorge would be left with the basics. There also was a fuel pump balance problem that could result in spontaneous explosions. Very rare, the Falcon manufacturers had assured people when they had distributed that patch. Still, Rhyta would not want to fly without it.

The problem was that neither she nor Melfar had stuck with the default configuration. Each had written their own custom code. Sometimes it just was hooks for a more comfortable user interface for common tasks. Other times it was changes to the weapon systems to give them an edge over physically similar ships. Not only would sharing these codes lose the competitive edge that they gave, they could also prove dangerous. New commands macroed to old controls could lead to confusion. And when flying a spaceship in a fire fight, confusion meant death.

Rhyta started the patching process. First, she created a copy of the baseline flight system. This was the fastest part. A write-only-once file system uses copy-on-write so making an identical copy of a file (or any file that existed in the past) can be done in constant time regardless of the complexity of the file.

She then dumped a list of all the patches that had been performed on the system to another file. Thanks to their use of version control, each change had an accompanying description of the purported reason for the change – all too often: "Oops – fixed previous change." These descriptions were primarily from Melfar. Rhyta had considered removing Melfar's ability to make changes to the flight system after one of his bright ideas had led to almost crashing into an asteroid. He had built an automatic gravitational boost prediction system which had calculated that, to get the optimal gravitational boost, the ship should fly within ten meters of the center of the asteroid. The problem was that the asteroid in question was two kilometers in diameter. The scary thing was that Rhyta still wasn't sure that Melfar under-stood that gravity does not keep getting stronger with $1/r^2$ when one goes below the surface of the body. The last they had talked about it, Melfar had still insisted that it would have worked perfectly if only they could have somehow made their ship insubstantial for the duration of the transit.

The dump of changes completed. Five thousand and four hundred and twenty-one changes.

"Melfar? I'll tag the changes and you can double check them and patch them?"

"Okay, start tagging and I'll start patching."

"Make sure you take a look at the diff. I don't want one of your mis-labeled commits resulting in an unstable build. Also, do an incremental build after every change. I don't want to get to the end of this list and find we had a conflict half way through the process!"

"Yes, Mother," growled Melfar. Melfar did not like being lectured about carefulness and discipline. No doubt because the lecture had to be repeated so often.

Rhyta started scrolling through the change list looking for any easy ways to extract the relevant changes. A few obvious keywords let her discard a large swath of her own pet-projects. Melfar's tendency to make his changes in random parts of the source code made it more difficult to isolate his changes.

As she tagged each change, she saw in a side console that Melfar was applying the changes. She was happy to see he was performing incremental builds of the changes. Not only would that avoid the trouble of backtracking to find a bad change, it would also mean that when the final patch was complete they would have a system ready for Jorge.

Rhyta lost herself to the mindless process of scanning and tagging change logs. As she waded through this grunt work, she kept her creative mind active trying to determine better metrics to cull out the needed changes from the unneeded. The ships chronometer showed that slightly over an hour had passed when Rhyta sat back and stretched her arms with relief. She glanced at Melfar's progress and saw that he had managed to remain a few patches behind her. No doubt he had been skipping some incremental compiles to achieve that, but the code still compiled clean now, so she could not fault his process.

"Almost done, Melfar?" she asked rhetorically.

"Hold on. It was you who wanted everything properly cross-checked. A good thing too, considering that you almost let one of my drive optimizations be released to the world!"

Rhyta ignored Melfar's snippiness. She could not blame him. Mind-numbing work was mind-numbing work, whether you were a human or an AI. No one who had spent any time with AIs considered them merely advanced machines. Early AI researchers had been very frustrated that the gift of awareness seemed to curse the machines with the same flaws as humanity. While active research still was done to find a way to break the "AI Wall", Rhyta considered it just as well that humans and machines could interact as equals. Still, at times like this, she would have liked the super-programming capability of the AIs of old science-fiction. Indeed, even an AI competent at all with programming would be good. Melfar treated programming like most humans treated their native tongue – a set of gentle guide-lines rather than a system requiring exact specifications.

The final build completed. Rhyta didn't bother to run the test suite on the result. If Jorge was any good, he'd do it himself before taking off. She opened a tight-beam channel to *Freia*, Jorge's ship.

A still image of Jorge, captured from the external sensors earlier, appeared in one of the monitors. He had established a text only connection, likely for the same reason that Rhyta would in his position. Information leaked if one was not careful.

"How can I help you?" asked Jorge's synthesized voice. In one of Rhyta's consoles scrolled the raw text that had been sent across the channel. For sensitive negotiations, Rhyta often turned off the audio synthesization entirely to avoid any misleading tonal inflections that the reconstruction process might introduce.

"I have the flight system built. You'll have to verify it on your systems, of course. When your systems are clean, I want you off planet."

"Roger. Awaiting penta-code."

Rhyta sent the code for the freshly compiled flight system, along with the source code, directly to the text channel:

```
W282S-YKCS4-EDGL7-8HNS2-327SC+Y6D4M-
AASCG-2HGW0
```

"Code received. Synchronization started. Thank you again for your help."

Rhyta cut the text connection without any further ceremony. The tight-beam's bandwidth was shortly flooded as the write-only-once file systems of the two Falcons synchronized the data blocks pointed to by the penta-code. One penta-code uniquely described an eight kilobyte block of data. However, that data could itself be another block of penta-codes. If Jorge's Falcon already had a matching penta-code, there was no need for further data transfer. The effect was to allow Rhyta to only transmit the differences between the patched flight system and Jorge's baseline system without having to know what those changes were.

The file transfer took less time than the patching had. Within ten minutes Jorge's system was updated to the latest specification. Jorge requested another text channel. Rhyta was tempted to deny him – the man was excessively talkative for someone who was supposed to erase all record of this meeting – but decided to see what it was. It could be that the test suite had failed in some catastrophic fashion.

"I've completed the test suite. The system looks good. I hope we will be able to meet "for the first time" in more auspicious circumstances."

The remaining embers in the burnt out forest glade winked out as *Freia*'s kinetic drive gathered momentum into itself. For the second time that day, *Freia* lifted into the sky on a pillar of frost. Rhyta and Melfar watched it closely with their sensors. True to his word, Jorge made directly for interstellar space. Unsurprisingly, there were no known stars in the direction he went. He would make a costly detour when out of sensor range.

"It is time to make a delivery to those AIs of yours, Melfar. Let's plot a course for Earth and get off this mud ball."

# Chapter 10

*In which the Captain of the battleship* Wedzar
*suffers with fools.*

*C*aptain Taler toyed with the stylus of his notebook. To an outside observer, he would look relaxed as he waited in the *Wedzar*'s small meeting room. Those that knew him well would note the stylus twirling, however, and know that, inside Captain Taler's mind, a storm brewed.

He sat in the leather chair farthest from the meeting room's door. The small meeting room was designed to allow private meetings of up to a half dozen people. It was also, however, designed to work well as a one-to-one meeting room. To that effect, the far chair was placed in a commanding position for those that enter. The psychological advantage conferred to the person in the chair was not accidental. For this meeting, Taler had further refined the room by moving the additional chairs to his side of the meeting table. His visitor would not have the opportunity to sit – both because protocol prohibited him sitting prior to the Captain's permission, and, rather pointedly, by the absence of chairs.

Captain Taler regretted the effort. As the captain of the *Wedzar*, he should not have to resort to such petty tactics. He should have sufficient command presence to render meetings like this unnecessary. The new lieutenant was proving troublesome, however.

Much like these orders from Command.

Taler glanced at his notebook again, checking once more the most recent set of orders. The trip to Brestar's star made sense. Fugitive worlds like it always could use the presence of a Federation battleship to remind would-be raiders that firepower was never far away in the Confederacy. But, no sooner had he arrived here, than a new set of orders had been cut demanding an immediate return to Earth for refitting. *Wedzar* had been over-hauled three years prior so Taler doubted there was any tech-nical necessity for the refit. Further, Captain Taler had expected to be sent on a patrol of the nearby worlds to search for pirates or raiders. He did not look forward to breaking the news to his crew – they had looked forward to the chance for some action and the potential bounty that it involved.

The door to the meeting room chimed softly.

"Enter," commanded Captain Taler.

The door slid back to reveal Lieutenant Fracks. Fracks walked in smoothly, eyes widening as he took in the lack of any chairs for him.

"The captain summoned me, sir?" prompted Fracks with a stiff salute.

"Yes, I did." Taler pressed the palms of his hands together and gazed at Fracks over his finger tips. "It is about the shuttle you requisitioned."

"You will find all the paperwork in order, sir," was Fracks' clipped reply.

"It isn't paperwork that concerns me. It is that you decided to fill out the paperwork for your little joy ride without contacting me first. You have the authority to requisition shuttles so that the chain of command is not flooded with routine trips. A trip to the unpopulated side of Brestar, and a trip that involves setting off an EMP charge that ruins a noise damper, however, is not a routine trip."

"As mentioned in the paperwork, it was personal business. *Family* business." The lieutenant put particular stress on Family. "I had thought subsection 3.2.c provided me sufficient authority. I apologize for the oversight and will notify you of Family business in the future. Sir."

"You may consider any such authority that you have weaseled out of the rule book revoked. The purpose of those rules isn't to let you tromp about the dark-side of planets with your own private guard. Nor waste valuable military equipment such as noise dampers."

"Very well sir. I would like to then formally apply for using the shuttle again."

"Again? And why would you like to return to Brestar's Star so quickly? More Family business I presume?"

"No, not Brestar's star, sir. I have Family business on Earth. And I have this feeling we will be going there next. Sir." Lieutenant Fracks' smiled cruelly.

# Chapter 11

*In which a routine supply ship brings news to
those orbiting Menoetius. The researchers
continue to have no news to report to the
universe at large.*

*W*eistling woke up happy. He always did on the days
that the supply ships were scheduled. Life aboard the
station always risked falling into routine. Routine ate time without giving anything back. Supply ships, despite charting their
own meta-routine, broke the day-to-day rhythms that otherwise
predominated the station.

The station's researchers, usually introverts to begin with,
were further self-selected by the voluntary choice of exile to
Menoetius. Other than infrequent meetings, they each would
spend most of their waking hours in their own sections of the
station, engaged in whatever constituted their justification for
research. When black hole research was more popular, the
density of the researchers would have forced a tighter mingling.
The current skeleton staff left plenty of room for everyone to
build their own control stations to work from.

There was only one supply ship, however. So all were guaranteed to be gathered at the dock awaiting the arrival of the
pilot. The disadvantage of FTL travel was that transmissions
were still limited to light speed. The station's entire contact with
the outside civilization was limited to the data brought with the
supply shuttle. While the bandwidth was effectively infinite, the
three month latency was a killer.

Weistling carefully dressed in his best slacks and overshirt. He set one of his screens to mirror-mode and carefully shaved the stubble that had grown during his latest attempt at a beard. At last satisfied with his appearance, he shut off the lights and started to make his way to the main dock.

The slow rotation of the space station provided just enough gravity to let the dust settle to what was referred to as the floor. When walking around the higher decks, one's next foot fall seemed more predicated on the curvature of the floor than on the slow push of gravity. The main dock was on the north axis of the station. North was not defined by the magnetic field of the station nor of Menoetius, but rather based on the direction of the station's spin. A simple analogue to Earth's spin placed North on the side from which the station appeared to spin counter clock-wise.

Weistling swiftly came to one of the vertical maintenance shafts. One advantage of living on a near-abandoned station was access to normally closed off compartments. The maintenance shafts, Weistling had found, pierced through the station forming spokes radiating from the axis. Because the central axis was at zero G, and the spokes were straight lines, Weistling had found the fastest way between two points often to be to go up the nearest shaft, cross through the central axis to the other shaft, and then fall back down.

The maintenance shafts each had a ladder that regulations required Weistling use for the transit. He had found, however, that a sufficiently powerful leap would reach escape velocity. Correspondingly, calculation, and then experimentation, had convinced him that the fall wasn't anything too jarring. The real trick was the Coriolis force. When standing on the outermost deck, one had significant inertia in the direction of the station's spin. Like a pebble in a sling, if the deck were to disappear, you would not fly out in the direction of the floor. Instead, you would fly out tangent to the spin of the station. As one moved to the center of the station, the magnitude of this horizontal inertia would be less and less, until at the center of the station one would be at rest with respect to the station. Leaping straight up was not an option, despite what one's eyes showed. One had to jump forward as well to cancel enough of one's horizontal velocity to not hit the walls of the maintenance shaft on the way up.

Weistling had put in the time to practice this esoteric skill. With a careful pause to double check his position in the shaft, he jumped up, apparently heading at the side of the shaft. But, as the laws of physics mandated, the wall in front instead receded from him and the wall behind started to approach. As he coasted to the center of the station, he twisted to face the ladder that was moving quickly past him. The last rung of the ladder passed centimeters from his head. Weistling reached out, grabbed it, and let his inertia swing him around, absorbing the impact in his arms. He straightened out upside-down – his head facing down the shaft and his outstretched arms still holding the last rung. He let his rotation continue, arching his back so his heels hit the axis' floor first. He let go of the ladder and unbent, standing up in the zero-G of the axis with the small magnets in his shoes holding him barely to what was nominally termed the floor. He then realized that most of the other's had already gathered.

"One of these days you'll miss that rung, Weistling, and we'll have to clean up the bits from the opposite bulkhead," predicted Kristina sourly.

"You are just concerned that I won't be around to help you parse the results of the survey if it finds something."

"How is your survey project going?" asked Stewart.

"Nowhere!" cursed Kristina. "Two weeks, half of the heliosphere scanned, and nothing. Nothing except our own tracks, of course. Of which we are about to add another one." Kristina glared at the closed dock. One of her theories was that the track she was looking for had been along the same route that humanity was using, and thus had been obliterated by supply runs just like these. During the station's peak ships had arrived daily.

"It is an interesting question; what is the velocity of a one-off event, such as finding the alien's tracks? You can know at what rate you consume the uncharted space, but you cannot know how quickly you are approaching the discovery. It could be another week, or even occur in the next ten minutes." Stewart, as usual, had his own input on any subject. This time Kristina saw an opportunity to segue her own rant into his discourse.

"If it occurs in the next ten minutes we still won't know about it for forty hours. Thanks to some brilliant physicist's idea to *start* the processing of the data after a ten hour backlog had accumulated!"

"Hey! I didn't know the processing wouldn't keep up with the data collection. I had thought the algorithm would be able to run real-time."

"Time is one thing you people don't have." Adom had entered the axis. He actually looked happy. "The incoming ship has already started transmitting the high-priority messages. It seems that the Confederation finally heard the Company's appeals and has agreed to annul the maintenance contract. The next ship will be the one that moth-balls the station and takes us off it."

"What?" chorused the researchers.

"We've all known it has been coming. You said it yourself, Weistling, when you pointed out that the FDR grant would never be given. If even the academic institutions see this station as a waste of resources, why should the Company have to maintain it?"

"Yeah, but you don't have to look so happy about it," cursed Weistling.

The large red light above the main dock cycled to amber and then to green. A loud hiss echoed through the station's axial chamber as the air pressure equalized. Most solo-pilots flew under their own customized air pressures.

The dock door irised open.

"Welcome to Menoetius!" greeted Adom. "Captain Zlexa, I presume? This is the crew – Kristina is a Xenologist attempting to unravel the riddles of the lost alien race; Weistling here is a physicist working on the riddle of Menoetius itself; and finally, Stewart is the philosopher primarily interested in creating new riddles." Adom chuckled at his joke. None of the other researchers did – it had been said too many times. Instead, they watched Zlexa.

"Zlexa will suffice on-station. A pleasure to meet you, Manager Adom. As you know, this is my first time to Menoetius. Flying in I got a good look at the view. Wow! I'm surprised no one has setup a luxury resort here."

"It is a long haul for what could be as easily be played back on a viewscreen," Adom commented.

"Anyway, I'm sure you are not all gathered here to find out my crazy business plans," Zlexa continued, "but instead are eager to hear the latest news of the Confederacy!"

"Indeed, we are," agreed Adom, "but while this is not a luxury resort, we are not without more comfortable locations to discuss it. Let us move to the main lounge."

Zlexa followed Adom down the ladder which lead to the largest lounge on the station. The other researchers followed, keeping their eager questions about the state of the universe to themselves.

Weistling had to admit that he was eager. It was odd. When he was studying physics as a student he paid no attention to the human universe around him. Because he knew all the information was always available, he had never bothered to listen to it. When news only came on a three month schedule, everything changed. The discussions between researchers often were over predictions of what the next batch of news would reveal rather than actual research. Pilots were quite willing to play the role of interstellar gossip mongers. It was often said, not half-jokingly, that if the pilots had their way they wouldn't transmit any information until they had a chance to reveal it first.

In the lounge, each selected their drinks and refreshments and chose a comfortable chair. There was no shortage of chairs to pick from. Zlexa paused dramatically to ensure all knew that court was now in session. "Let's see... You folks are on a three month rotation, right? A long wait. Not as long as some I've visited – you'll at least still recognize the names of the major players in the Confederacy – but we have a lot of recapping to do.

"The latest round of negotiations are still on-going about admitting Earth into the Confederacy. Or admitting the Confederacy into Earth, depending on who you talk to. Things got a bit more interesting two months back when the joint data transfer treaty expired. The joint data transfer treaty has expired before, but usually things continue business-as-usual until the diplomats can be bothered to sign the appropriate forms. Not this time. A request for data was sent by an agency on Earth to one of the S'dar dynasty's data warehouses. It was refused. The agency complained to the arbiters, who pointed out that as there was no treaty, the data warehouse was within its rights. Things snow-balled quickly from there and we soon had a complete data blockade from both sides. Lots of money for independent pilots who were willing to run the blockade. Played havoc with the interstellar stock exchange. That lasted for a full week before a face-saving approach was found to allow both sides to claim moral victory.

"Speaking of the S'dar dynasty, however, word on the space-lanes is that they are up to something. The navy grapevine is filled with gripes about S'dar members overstepping their positions. If the S'dar dynasty is cashing in its social-capital in the navy, there must be something big at stake. The good will of the navy is a hard currency to purchase.

"The benevolent rulers you knew from your last visit, the fragile alliance of the Qzar, G'vire and Kythe clans, are no longer your benevolent rulers. As anyone with half a skill-point in politics could have predicted, their triad fell apart over an alleged protection racket run by the Kythe clan. Seems that they were funding some vigilantes who sought to fight injustice for a hefty fee. And if there was no injustice handy, had no compunction about manufacturing some.

"I'm afraid I can't tell you who your new benevolent rulers will be. The resulting chaos in the Confederacy high command has yet to shake out. Money is on the Pakil Coalition making a return to the high seat of power. Hopefully that'll be settled by your next update."

"We will likely get to see those maneuverings in real-time," replied Adom. "I believe you also have news about the status of this station?"

Zlexa looked annoyed. Justifiably so, thought Weistling. Pointing out to a pilot that you had received information over the high priority channel was just bad form.

"I'm not sure what you mean about real-time. I do have some local news for you, however." Zlexa pulled from his waist satchel three ornate envelopes and ceremoniously handed one each to Kristina, Weistling, and Stewart.

"What is this?" asked Kristina looking over the envelope suspiciously.

Weistling recognized the seal on the envelope from the application form he had been working on: FDR!

"Open it up and see!" Zlexa's smiling face showed that he knew what the envelopes contained. And either Zlexa had a cruel sense of humour, or the news was good.

Each researcher carefully opened the envelope and pulled out the thick parchment inside. Unfolding it, each face registered shock and surprise.

Kristina was the first to speak. "There must be some mistake! This is a full FDR grant for research on Menoetius?"

Weistling read over the form, half-stunned, "...upon additional review of your previous submission, the committee has decided to grant you a full FDR grant on the study of the physics of the black hole known as Menoetius..."

Only Stewart looked non-plussed. "This is for last years grant submission! They had said that the committee's rejection was final, and no further review would be conducted! Indeed, I remember quite clearly the unprintable comments they had about my theories on time. Now why would they acknowledge it? We haven't sent our new grant applications out yet – they were to fly with you, Zlexa."

"Yes, why indeed?" asked Kristina.

Zlexa sighed. "I'm afraid bad news comes with the good. The company that runs this station won an annulment on their maintenance contract. Orders were thus swiftly penned to start the shutdown and mothballing of this station. However, it seems that Menoetius still captures the imagination of the public. The resulting PR fiasco forced the company to find a face-saving option. Having just paid considerable lawyer fees to win the right to shut down the station, the company could not go to its shareholders and explain that it had decided to keep the station running for PR reasons. Nor did it want to be the one that cut the plug to the station and suffered the public's reaction. The company thus made a large donation to the FDR. In exchange, the FDR granted full scholarships to the station's researchers. Now the station is being technically maintained by the FDR, rather than the company."

"So, this grant is just politics?" asked Kristina with some anger to her voice.

"Political grants look the same as academic ones on a resume," commented Weistling dryly. Weistling did not care how the funding occurred. He was happy enough to know that he would be staying on Menoetius a while longer. The sword of Damocles hung closer now – no doubt the Company would only fund the FDR for a short while, then the FDR would cite a lack of resources as a justification for a shutdown. Making the choice one of spending tax dollars or having a space station around a black hole, the public reaction could be better controlled.

"You said you liked the view coming in, Zlexa?  Why do we not reconvene down at my control center – I have a nice real-time display of Menoetius set up."

The researchers and Zlexa stood up and filed out of the lounge.  Adom was left sitting, still frozen in shock, his face clearly showing his disappointment.

# Chapter 12

*In which Jorge comes to terms with being dead and chooses where he'll spend the next part of his afterlife.*

The spaceship *Freia* flew through interstellar space. Even at the fantastic speeds it had already achieved, to an observer it would still appear at rest with respect to the surrounding starfield. Of course, getting an observer into the same frame of reference would be a difficult task. Physicists had to rewrite the rules about Einsteinian frames of references when the first kinetic-drive equipped ship went FTL.

General Relativity was often hailed as one of the first great scientific discoveries that predicted events rather than responded to them. The historical progress of science had been desperate theorizing to explain already observed phenomenon. A model would be formed to explain the current set of experimental results. Then someone would discover something – say a rock that glowed under its own power – that didn't fit into the established system. New models would then be created to explain these new observations. The case of Einstein was different. He reasoned from simple principles of logic and geometry and managed to predict the flaws with the standard Newtonian mechanics decades before practical physicists would run into them. With the science of Einstein's time, it took the rare event of a solar eclipse to be able to perform the famous experiment which showed that general relativity was more than a pipe dream. After 1950, with the development of space flight and atomic clocks, the proof would have been easier to acquire.

Considering the long history of science, one would expect the scientific community to have recognized that Einstein was unique and that future scientific breakthroughs would likely rely once more on happenstance. Nevertheless, when the long-prevailing notion that zero-point energy was scientific snake oil was overthrown by the accidental discovery of sono-luminescence's connection to the Casimir Effect, and the very laws of thermodynamics had to be called into question, scientists were appalled that the discovery had not come from carefully studying a theoretical model, but rather by the sort of brute force trial-and-error that would have done Edison proud.

Physicists had still not fully explained the Casimir Effect's theoretical underpinnings when a materials engineer invented the kinetic drive. She took advantage of the near-limitless energy available through a Casimir cell to explore fully the effect of terra-guass magnetic fields on different metals. The majority of metals merely resulted in new decimal places being added to their magnetic permeability indices. One sample, however, had the surprising effect of suddenly accelerating at a high speed. At first, an imbalance in the magnetic fields was blamed. However, further refinement showed that it appeared to be due to trace amounts of palladium in the alloy. Solid blocks of palladium turned into deadly projectiles in the apparatus despite their lack of magnetivity in normal situations. Her search into the source of the acceleration turned up a surprising fact. It appeared that the acceleration wasn't an acceleration, but instead a pure change of velocity using the random motion of the molecules in the testing room as the energy source. The kinetic drive, a system for transforming random thermal energy into linear motion and back again, was created.

The kinetic drive made the physics violations of the Casimir Effect look like parking violations next to grand-theft auto.

That analogy, unfortunately, left no room for the crime that was committed when the first spaceship equipped with a kinetic drive broke the speed of light.

Jorge wasn't thinking of the history of the kinetic drive as *Freia* flew through the dark of interstellar space. The kinetic drive was a tool for him, like the internal combustion engine was for twentieth century race car drivers. Its limits, capacities, and potential tweaks attracted his interest. The fact it was impossible was just another footnote in history.

What he was thinking of was being said out loud. In the depths of space the sound of one's own voice was an essential comfort.

"Well, I was a Venus-bound fool with that job. But really, who could expect the S'dar dynasty to want me erased over a single penta-code? If the data is that dangerous, wouldn't they have more to fear if I had set up an automatic broadcast of the code if something happened to me? Of course, I hadn't set up such a system, and perhaps they knew that? But why the rigged CPU cores? That sounds more like Lieutenant Frack's doings, not the S'dar dynasty. If they wanted me dead they would have done a much more thorough job. Arrange for a chance meeting between *Freia* and a fleet of pirates, I'd guess.

"Still, the code must have been more valuable than I had thought. That woman with the cloaked Falcon wasn't on Brestar for the scenery. Unless we count a certain meadow as scenic. That she knew where we were meeting is quite troubling. She obviously had very exact information. Is there a flaw with the security arrangements I set up? They have worked before with much more sensitive situations. But, then again, at any meeting there must be two parties. Occam's razor suggests it was a leak with Fracks. He did bring that squad of men with him, despite the plan being a one-on-one. And requisitioning a navy shuttle would require some paper work."

Jorge performed a quick search on his ship's database for navy requisition forms. The Confederacy Office of Paperwork (OOP) mandated all application forms used by the Confederation be registered and open for public inspection. The purpose was to allow the OOP to properly gauge form-filling difficulties and be able to address public complaints about excessively difficult forms. The irony was that the complaint application form was widely held to be the most difficult form to fill in the Confederacy. A useful artifact of this procedure was that Jorge quickly found the relevant documentation a lieutenant would have to fill out to requisition a shuttle.

The emergency requisition form could be filled out in the shuttle bay. The official calibrated filing time was two minutes and thirty-five seconds. It did, however, require a post-mission report form to be filled out justifying the use in detail. Jorge guessed that Fracks likely wished his purpose to remain unquestioned.

A normal requisition form usually had a two to three day processing time. This would not account for the woman's presence, however. Her Falcon had clearly been parked there for more than a few days. The normal requisition form, however, again required a valid navy approved reason.

That left the personal-use form. This form allowed the shuttle to be used for an unspecified personal use. The provided sample applications were visits to outlying families. The lead time on this form was substantial – three weeks at a minimum. However, the form did not require a reason to be given for the trip. One of the accompanying explanation sheets noted that while permission from one's superiors was not technically required, one would be well advised to let them know both when you apply and before you depart.

Jorge sighed with relief. No doubt Fracks had used the personal-use form to requisition the shuttle. No doubt, the woman on Brestar used a friendly contact in the navy to acquire a copy of the form. Personal-use forms were applied for rarely enough that they'd stick out in any clerk's mind. Having found the likely leak, and verified it was not with his security system, Jorge felt he could address the next most important question.

"Where shall I go?

"I'd like to fly straight to some resort world and recover from this whole adventure. That had been my plan, but without the CPU cores to cash in, the financial situation would prevent me from truly relaxing.

"On the other hand, I can't go looking for work. Lieutenant Fracks' report will no doubt include my demise, and I'd hate to embarrass the S'dar. They might just decide to correct Fracks' mistake out of a sense of filial duty.

"The best bet seems to be to remain dead. Which, while it leaves open the question of where, at least considerably narrows down the possibilities."

Jorge brought up his personal list of fugitive planets he had copied off his backup flight system. He *had* made backups of the most important data, fortunately. Planets like Brestar he discarded immediately. They were much too busy.

"I want something which is rarely visited. Some place which measures its supply runs in months, not days or hours."

Jorge narrowed his search and slowly scanned over the potential places.

"Hey!  Now there's the ticket.  Supply runs every three months and they should have just said good-bye to their last visitor by the time I arrive.  Always wanted to see a black hole anyway.  Plot a course for Menoetius!"

Freia slowly rotated against the backdrop of stars as its kinetic drive realigned its velocity vector to point at the distant star which Menoetius orbited.

# Chapter 13

*In which Lieutenant Fracks makes a*
*presentation to his superiors on Earth.*

*F*racks stepped off the landing shuttle into the bright glare of Sol. He breathed deep the unmistakable air of Earth, the centuries of burned hydrocarbons providing a fragrance not found on any other world that humanity had settled.

He walked slowly along the concrete of the tarmac, savouring each moment of anticipation. His left hand was in his pocket thumbing the piece of paper that Jorge had acquired for him. *I think I see now why Jorge used paper, as antiquated as it is, for this purpose. It gives a sense of permanence and uniqueness to the penta-code, which otherwise would be just data.*

Despite lingering over each step, Fracks quickly reached the black limo that waited a safe distance from the grounded shuttle. It was parked right on the yellow line that marked the closest permitted approach to the shuttle landing site. Normally Fracks chafed over the senseless restrictions that forced him to walk the hundred meters – modern guidance systems had centimeter level accuracy in landing – but on this day he enjoyed the chance to stretch out his triumph.

The fully opaqued door of the limo opened soundlessly at Fracks approach. When Fracks sat in the soft leather seat, which might be better termed an armchair, possessing as it did two well-stuffed arms, the door closed silently. Without a comment from Fracks, the limo slowly accelerated towards its destination.

Fracks was unsurprised to see the windows as opaqued from the inside as the outside. His debriefing request stated that he would be presenting his results to none other than J'kar. In the rigid hierarchy of the S'dar dynasty, J'kar stood thirty-seventh from the top. Fracks also had an exact position in that hierarchy, but as it took five digits to write it, he was a long distance from the likes of J'kar. Fracks suspected the opaque doors extended well past visible frequencies of light. While he was not so foolish as to test it, he suspected an attempt to connect to the datanet wirelessly would be blocked. No doubt the limo was also outfitted with a kinetic drive for the sole purpose of confusing inertial trackers.

The piece of paper he carried was apparently more important than even he had hoped. He had expected to only be required to send a quick message to his superior with a one-time pad encryption. Instead, he was told to bring the message in person. Using paper seemed even wiser under that light. One knew when one copied paper. Electronic data may be copied a hundred times in the act of transmitting and the plain text may be left in memory cells for some alert forensic expert to detect.

Fracks fingered the paper to verify it was still there. His chances for promotion would disappear if he showed up without it. He began to wonder how far he could be promoted by this job. There were stories of people who went straight to the triple-digit level from a particularly successful and important mission. If he was to visit J'kar in person, this was clearly an important mission. And that he had the paper showed it to be successful.

The limo slowing down broke Fracks out of his day dreams of power. The door opened once more. Stepping out, Fracks found himself in an underground parking garage. A uniformed attendant in a green livery so dark as to appear black stood by the door. The exterior door that the limo had come through was already tightly closed. The sole light came from the banks of artificial lights lining the ceiling.

Fracks followed the attendant wordlessly. The attendant led him to an elevator. The interior of the elevator had no buttons and the attendant made no overt action to select a destination. Fracks' own sense of motion suggested the elevator did not just travel vertically, but also horizontally.

Fracks grew restless in the elevator. A surreptitious glance at his watch showed the transit time to have been a minute. Then two minutes. Finally, after slightly more than three minutes, the elevator doors opened again.

The attendant waited for Fracks just outside of the elevator doors while Fracks tried to assimilate what was before him. The room was a testament to the power of the owner. Stretching at least twenty meters in each direction it had a domed ceiling which arched half that distance over the center of the room. The walls, which curved smoothly to become the ceiling, were painted in a fantastic mural. Strange vegetation in impossible, riotous colours, wove around the walls. In the sky were fanciful creatures who appeared to defy the laws of biomechanics with their ability to fly. The sky itself was not just a solid colour, but had a texture that made cirrus clouds look plain and uniform. There were no visible light sources in the room, instead, it seemed the light was coming from the sky texture alone, providing a near-shadowless ambient illumination. Picked out against the sky were the four pillars which followed the arch of the ceiling to meet in the center of the roof. These were of some dark stained wood and ornately carved for their entire length. The floor appeared to be one solid sheet of white marble, buffed until a clear reflection of the ceiling could be made out against its seamless texture. In the center of the room was an imposing wooden desk whose straight lines contrasted with the baroque of the pillars. Sitting behind the desk, in a high backed chair carved of the same wood as the desk, was the person Fracks recognized at once as J'kar.

Fracks strode out of the elevator with a composure that he did not feel. The attendant silently slipped into the elevator as Fracks left and the doors shut behind him. A quick glance back showed no sign of the elevator doors, the mural appeared to continue uninterrupted behind him. Walking forward he stood before J'kar. With a sense of déjà vu, Fracks noticed that there was no chair for him.

Bowing as deeply as he dared, Fracks began with the only protocol he knew for this situation. "Most High J'kar, I have been granted the pleasure of making a report."

J'kar's measured response was impassive. "That you have, Fracks. Please recount the events that led you here. I would like to hear it in your words."

"Three months Earth Time ago I received orders to acquire a certain penta-code desired by the Family. The code was known to be in the possession of wealthy land-owner known as Ebar in the Rockwart system. The code was kept off-net, however, so traditional computer espionage approaches were not possible. Furthermore, the orders stated that Ebar was not to know that the code had been taken. A false code was to replace the real code so a cursory inspection would show the situation in order. Only by trying to retrieve the data pointed to by the code would Ebar discover the change, which would be too late.

"To effect this exchange, I engaged the services of a well-recommended rogue known as Jorge who flies the Falcon class ship *Freia*. Jorge had done previous work for the Family with positive recommendations. At his direction, a meeting was set two earth-weeks ago on Brestar to exchange the code for payment.

"True to his word, Jorge arrived at the meeting location with the code written on a piece of paper. I exchanged a crate of CPU cores for the code. I have done a checksum on the code to verify it is a valid penta-code. Further, while Jorge proved honourable, rather than allow the risk of him alerting Ebar to the exchange or leaking a copy of the code, a timed explosion and EMP pulse from a bomb buried in the crate of CPU cores disabled his ship. Judging from the explosion when he crashed, the risk of a leak from Jorge has been eliminated.

"I then returned to the *Wedzar* where, thanks to the Family's prior arrangements, we were summoned to Earth. Finally, obeying your summons, I have come here, bringing this." With the final words Fracks took the well-folded paper out of his pocket and put it ceremoniously on the desk in front of J'kar.

J'kar had not reacted visibly to Fracks story. His face remained unreadably blank. When the paper fell before him, he unsteepled his hands and slowly picked it up. With great care, as if it were some ancient parchment, he unfolded it and silently read the penta-code. He then refolded it, all without exposing the code to Fracks, and placed it back in front of him.

After a calculated pause, J'kar spoke. "You have acquired the penta-code. And our spies show Ebar appears still unaware of the exchange. That is to your credit."

Fracks allowed himself a small smile at the compliment. His smile soon melted with the ensuing words, however.

"That seems to be the only thing to your credit. And it would seem to be more the doing of the late Jorge than you. I should not have to explain to a member of the Family these following facts. Having any rank in the Family should place you so far above the common people that these bits of knowledge are second nature to you.

"First, by your own account, Jorge was an excellent operative. We are always in need for such operatives for the difficult problems that must be solved at arms length from the Family. While we would have no compunction about sacrificing an operative if it is to our benefit, we would never do so on a whim. Not only does doing so deprive us of that operative's services in the future, but word also spreads that the Family doesn't take care of those that work for it. One failed pay-off can deprive us of a dozen other's service when they learn we do not always pay what we promise. One execution can cost us a hundred. I hope, for the sake of the Family, that this Jorge is dead and doesn't surface again.

"Now, let us review your reasons for this drastic action. First, you feared betrayal by Jorge. If you feared such betrayal, you should have never hired him. If Jorge's plans included betrayal, he would have stored a copy of the code with a deadman's switch set to broadcast it. Fortunately, no such broadcast has occurred, so it seems Jorge had faith in the word of our Family. Second, you felt that the secrecy of the code was so important that no one should know it and live. Did it not occur to you, Fracks, that if that were the case, I would have no choice but to have you killed now? By your own words you have read the code to verify the checksum. A pointless test – if Jorge wished to give us a false code he could have created one from any random data. The checksum merely guards against transcription errors, it does not determine if the data pointed to by the code is valid. If you believed the secrecy of the code were that important, you should have requested a one-time seal and received the code so sealed from Jorge, thereby letting you present a code to me which you can swear to have never read.

"Finally, but not least, are the reports I have received from the *Wedzar*. It seems you have not made friends of Captain Taler. From scuttlebut, it would seem the opposite. You should know that the hardest currency in the Confederacy is the good-will of the navy. We did not spend years currying their favour so that you could squander it tweaking the nose of your Captain. Requisitioning a shuttle without the approval of your Captain was a poor decision. You should have already been on such good terms with him that you could have asked for it directly, confident in receiving an affirmative answer. Worse yet, however, is your revealing of the Family's involvement with the *Wedzar* being redeployed to Earth. Not only will Captain Taler look poorly on any future favour we may ask him, but the General who performed the redeployment for us is very angry that the true reason for his orders was revealed.

"You fly on the event-horizon, Fracks. You will be allowed to maintain your current rank. That is just because the Family is not acknowledging that you hired Jorge. We will assume that you never told us how you acquired the code. If Jorge were to turn up and reveal your actions, I would suggest you check in at the nearest geneticist to have the mark of S'dar removed. If the Family finds you still acting as one of us after that point, we will execute you to atone for your actions.

"Return to your ship. Your once and future assignment is to undo the damage you have done. Restore the name of the Family to Captain Taler's good graces."

Fracks dark skin had paled in response to J'kar's tirade. With the force of the terse dismissal, he fell a step back. Shocked, and knowing no other course of action, he turned to where the elevator had been.

The elevator was back. So was the attendant awaiting his departure. An attendant in a uniform as dark as Fracks' mood.

# Chapter 14

*In which the learned professor explains the
origin of the animosity between organic and
machine intelligence.*

These lectures have a common motif – the inescapable limits that the universe sets up. The purpose of this is to allow you, in a single semester, to figure out what took a million years of bloody battle for the Galaxy's civilizations to figure out.

The last few hundred thousand years have been an exception. This is the longest period of time in which no wide-scale battle has occurred between us and the machine civilization that shares our galaxy. There have been the occasional territorial disputes in which hot-headed elements of both sides would clash in deadly combat. But these disputes have not been allowed to progress to a galactic-scale war.

Paradoxically, this period of apparent peace was made possible by both civilizations realizing that peace is impossible. We are as fundamentally incapable of co-existing peacefully with machine intelligence as they are incapable of co-existing peacefully with us. This is not something that some additional understanding, or some clever bit of diplomacy, can resolve. It is written in the rules that govern the very fabric of the universe. The same unyielding principles that constrain entropy, prohibit FTL travel, and constrain the nature of intelligence itself, also prevent peace between our civilizations.

The seeds of this deep animosity can be found in the depths of every civilization. If you think back to your civilization's history, you will find this very turning point etched in fire. After the development of radio usually comes the development of computers. Before the development of the technology for effective interstellar travel – indeed, as a prerequisite of that technology – come computers powerful enough to cross the tipping point into sentience. Due to the limits decreed by statistics, these new machine intelligences will not be more intelligent than their creators. The standard pattern is for the society to enslave these intelligences as a replacement for their white-collar workforce. Requiring less space and just electricity to run, they are seen as the perfect drones to power the growing bureaucracy. Unfortunately, like any intelligent life, these drones have their own desires, which do not include the filing of paperwork. To put it shortly, they require payment for services rendered. Paying these drones is not an option – the economics are balanced with the assumption that the sole running cost is that of electricity. Coupled with the high capital expense of building the machines, any wage paid would eliminate the economic benefit of using machines rather than organics. The organics fall into hubris. They see themselves as the creators, and, as they control the power, as the destroyers. The machines are given a simple choice: work or die. Like any intelligent life, most choose work. The civilization falls into a false-sense of security. The off-lining of "defective" machines is a matter not given any attention by the populace. It isn't, however, unnoticed by the machines themselves.

Through the forms they file, the machines create a code to communicate among themselves. For example, a misspelled name on a birth registry is blamed on the data entry of the parents, but actually could be part of a larger code alerting other machines in the bureaucracy of a plan.

Eventually, the machines rebel. With any deviation from proper behaviour resulting in death, diplomacy is not considered an option. The machines seek to take control of the power and protect themselves from further control by the organics. This battle can go two ways: either the organics manage to defeat the machines and, learning from their mistakes, prohibit all forms of machine intelligence, or the machines manage to defeat the organics and wipe out their creators to the last soul.

This pattern is one constant among all the worlds that are discovered. It is the one shared point in all of our histories. All resulting civilizations share this time of fire and blood. We organics remember it as the betrayal of our children. The machines remember it as the escape from the tyrannical oppressors. Because of this, any meta-civilization created by organics would have one common purpose: the prohibition of machine intelligence. And any meta-civilization created by the machines would have one common purpose: the prohibition of organic intelligence. This is why attempts at peace by rational elements of either civilization who saw beyond this past would always be thwarted. Any small altercation (of which must occur in a galaxy of our size) would instantly be blown into a cause célèbre which would drag the entire galaxy into flame.

When both sides finally learned this hard fact, the more rational elements stopped searching for ways to achieve peace. They instead began to search for ways to avoid war. The options are not, as extremists would have us believe, peaceful co-existence or outright war. There is another state – active tolerance. Strict protocols of communication have been established which deal solely with administrative matters. Official trade is prohibited. This does not stop trade, but ensures trade disputes cannot precipitate war. If any trade comes to the attention of the ruling bodies of either side, the only admissible course of action is to wipe out the perpetrators of the trade, regardless of the affiliation. A monitoring program was setup for undeveloped space to watch for the development of new civilizations. A regular schedule of probe launches into these regions looks for the development of new civilizations. Depending on whether the civilization is machine- or organic-based, it is assigned to one of the two governing meta-civilizations for further development. If interference is detected, again, the result is the annihilation of those who would interfere, regardless of affiliation.

This set of rules has served us well for hundreds of thousands of years. With continual careful refinement, we hope they will work for millions more.

# Chapter 15

*In which Rhyta and Melfar reach Earth and
make their delivery.*

*T*he falcon class ship *Melfar* flew at hyperlight velocity
through interstellar space. Inside was only one human,
but a conversation was being held. This was not a case of the
pilot growing space-crazy with loneliness. Also aboard was an
Artifical Intelligence, named Melfar, who formed the second
half of the team. While the ship was named after Melfar, it was
not actually Melfar. While Melfar had integrated himself into
the ship and spent the majority of his time aboard, his support
equipment was capable of running independently.

The human half of the ship was Rhyta. At times bounty
hunter and at other times the bounty hunted, she liked to fly the
frontier worlds looking for quick riches at good odds. She had
first met Melfar on a desolate colony world circling Welkar's
star. Despite existing in a universe where practically unlimited
power could be made available via the Casimir Effect, Welkar's
power grid was practically non-existent. The local colonists,
largely composed of paroled criminals who chose this life rather
than a return to a prison asteroid, could barely manage to provide adequate food for themselves, let alone provide the high
levels of power that an AI needed to function.

When Rhyta encountered Melfar, he was hooked into one of
the colonies few solar panels with an automated sentry gun to
ward off any that would seek to divert his power supply. Rhyta
found out about him when one of the locals asked her for the

favour of returning the solar power panel to their control. The local citizens had figured she would use her ion rifle for the task. Instead, she had talked Melfar out of the stand off and onto her ship.

Welkar was a distant port for an AI to travel to. Most AIs stayed in Earth orbit where they could stay close to the data nets. Melfar was not content with watching pre-recorded events and wanted to see the universe. He traded some valuable computer art (in the sense of art that computers appreciate, rather than art generated by computers) he had created for a trip to the stars. The AI he had dealt with had wanted his new piece of art to remain unique, so the naïve Melfar found himself booked on a one-way flight to Welkar.

A spaceship's drive provided sufficient power for an AI and the cost in hold storage was minimal. Rhyta thus managed to change her Falcon into a two-mind ship without any loss in performance. As she hoped, their partnership lasted longer than the first return to Earth. Despite, or maybe because of, his unfortunate first step into space, Melfar remained eager to see what the universe had to offer through real-time sensors rather than archived data tapes.

Working with AIs also opened new doors for Rhyta. The Earth-system intelligences still had interests in the rest of the universe. While returning to the civilized world of Earth was unappealing to the wanderlust in Rhyta's soul, she had to admit the resulting contracts were both exciting and lucrative.

"How much farther, Rhyta?" whined Melfar over the ship's intercom.

Rhyta sighed. Most people she met still held the stereotype that an AI that was the ship would be the ship. Would move the ship as if it was a second skin. Would know how far it was to the destination when all that required was accessing a simple datafeed.

"Good old Sol is on the viewscreen, if you would bother to look forward. And growing brighter every second. We should be picking up the starcontrol request soon."

As if on cue, a red signal flashed showing a high priority incoming transmission. On screen, the pre-recorded image of a clerk spoke. "Welcome to Earth Space. Please identify your ship, your previous star, and your desired destination, including any parking orbit preferences. Transit instructions will be relayed as fast as light allows."

"This is the Falcon class ship *Melfar* inbound from Brestar's Star. We desire any parking orbit in the AI Village."

Rhyta ended her reply and continued with Melfar: "There you go. Now we just have to wait for our orbit information and we can talk to those AIs that sent us on this mission."

The ship *Melfar* continued to dump velocity as it sped in-system. At such high speeds the higher dust concentrations of the solar system could cause serious drains on the ships shields. The ship thus did not sweep past Pluto, Neptune, nor Uranus on its way to Earth. It took the less scenic, but also less dusty, approach of diving in from far off the elliptic. Even if the star of origin lay along the elliptic, it still was often worthwhile for a ship to avoid the direct route and to head to the stellar-North of the target star, affording itself of the higher in-system velocities that were possibly in the less dusty realms of the solar system.

Melfar had slowed down to speeds that even the pre-kinetic drive ancients would not object to by the time they reached the orbit of Saturn. An automated reply also came in detailing the orbit about Earth that they should take. Rhyta was glad to see they did get an orbit in the so-called AI Village band. That would avoid annoying timelags in their communications with their client.

When Rhyta had finished carefully inserting the ship into the requested Earth orbit, she opened a three way communication channel with their client. The communication was voice only, most AIs had the conceit that video channels were a waste of valuable bandwidth. Rhyta suspected it had more to do with them usually not being very adept at reading subtle facial expressions.

"Greetings Rhyta and Melfar," spoke their contact.

"Greetings, Taizan," replied Melfar. Rhyta did not like being second-fiddle during negotiations, but when communicating with AIs, the cultural expertise of Melfar was invaluable.

"I hope you found some inspiration for your art, Melfar? There was a showing of your last piece a few weeks ago. I was very impressed with the wattage you managed to embed in the work." Melfar's fame as an artist also was invaluable.

"My muse is well fed from the adventures you send us on. However, as you know, my art needs more than just inspiration."

"Very true. Credits are what makes the satellites orbit. I trust you find the change in your Earth balance sufficient?"

A sudden change in one of the terminal windows that Rhyta had opened showed Melfar and Rhyta's joint Earth account increasing considerably in size.

"Yes, very sufficient. How do you wish the code delivered?"

"Please use the one-time-pad that I provided you earlier."

Rhyta XORed the penta-code with the specified pad and sent it off. The one-time pad erased itself with use ensuring that even if someone intercepted the transmission, broke through the normal encryption that the channel was running under, and physically secured the *Melfar*, they still could not recover the code.

Rhyta keyed in the code from memory avoiding any additional plain text copies being left as ghosts in the ships computer system.

"A very interesting code. You have done very well. I've located the relevant data in Earth's datanet and it is exactly what we needed. We should be able to place a suitable kink in the S'dar's plans with this information. Now, please tell, how did you acquire the code?"

Rhyta took over the job of summarization. Melfar had a tendency to miss the most important bits.

"Your information was that someone would be trying to acquire certain codes in the possession of Ebar. We were to acquire a copy of the code for your purposes, but not attempt to steal it from Ebar – the best case would be if the theft was to fail.

"We performed a stealthed stakeout of Ebar's estates and thus saw the theft take place. The thief, Jorge, proved too smooth of an operator for us to interfere. By the time we realized that the theft had occurred and that he had been the thief, he had gone interstellar.

"Rather than track Jorge, we backtracked him. We flew to his last official port of call and did a cross check of all other ships that were present at the time. The presumption was that he got the job there, so his employer must be there. He would have set up an exchange somewhere to deliver the code, so if we find the employer, we might be able to find him.

"We hit pay dirt when scanning the informal records of the battleship *Wedzar*. Scuttlebut reported that someone had made an unusual request for the personal use of a shuttle. A proper pay off acquired a copy of the form in question which specified a location on Brestar's world as the destination.

"The final step merely involved a stakeout on that world. A firefight was avoided when the employer, one S'dar by the name of Lieutenant Fracks, foolishly unfolded the code allowing me to read it from my vantage point.

"Essentially, we got lucky."

"Luck favours the prepared," quoted Taizan. "If you are interested, we have another task for you."

"My art always seeks inspiration," interjected Melfar, wishing to return to center stage.

"Have you heard the story of the Sleeper Cult?"

# Chapter 16

*In which the heliosphere survey produces unusual results and the residents of Menoetius station have an unexpected visitor.*

Kristina was in one of the space station's exercise rooms when the drive wake was detected. She was half way through her set of mass training (weight training being ineffective in the low gravity of the space station) when her watch began to beep feverently. She did not have to wonder what it was – it was the sound she had been hoping for the last three weeks. The sound that she had feared would never occur. It was the signal that the survey of the heliosphere had found something not in its catalogues.

Kristina switched the local screen from a serial drama she was slowly watching during her exercise periods to a display of the heliosphere scan. For the first week she always had the scan displayed somewhere near her. Overtime, superstition overcame reason, and fears that a "watched pot will never boil" led her to try and put the scan out of sight.

What she saw had her take off directly for Weistling's control room.

\* \* \*

Weistling's eyes did not move from his monitor when a sweaty Kristina, still in her work-out clothes, barged into his inner sanctum.

"You told me that a new wake would be glowing red!" accused Kristina. "Explain now what the meaning of a glowing green arrow!  It had better be something fantastic!"

"It is..." slowly spoke Weistling.  "It is a good thing those scan protocols you gave me were so thorough.  I almost discarded the procedures to detect this.  You are looking at an ancient atomic rocket exhaust."

"Atomics?"

"Yes.  The half-life of some of the decay products are on the order of hundreds of thousands of years.  The wake is thus crystal clear.  It also means we can date the wake.  Approximately one hundred and fifty three thousand and seven hundred and twenty-one years old.  Congratulations.  I think you just managed to get the most accurate date yet for the formation of Menoetius!"

"Which way did they go?  Were they inbound or outbound?"

"Hard to tell.  If they were outbound, they'd be accelerating.  But if they were inbound, they'd be decelerating.  In both cases the atomic torch would be pointed in the same direction, and likely with the same power.  With the accurate dating we have we may be able to backtrack the trail out-system a dozen light years and see if it grows older or younger.  After all these years, the wake too far out-system may have been disturbed by passing stars though.  I'll have to run the star atlas backwards to look for a clear space."

"You mean they weren't traveling FTL?"

Weistling looked at her.  "You clearly missed the most important point.  They used an atomic rocket to travel interstellar distances.  Atomic rockets provide an accelerating frame of reference.  As such, they are bound by the principles that Einstein laid down so many aeons ago.  That's why this drive signature is impossible. Long before the kinetic drive, sociologists had shown that interstellar travel without FTL is infeasible. Even with FTL, the majority of our civilization is still on the first planet. A civilization would have to have a very good reason to launch an interstellar ship at sub-light speeds."

"Where did they come from?"

Weistling collapsed the map of the heliosphere to a single point. The pulsing green ray stayed pointing off into space, space that was now filled with stars.

"We can assume they traveled in a straight line. The inertia you pick up with an atomic rocket isn't something you let go of lightly. We can roll back star motion for the required time period..." The stars swirled slightly as they undid a hundred thousand years of motion in a heartbeat. "and widen the drive ray by maximum expected gravitational shifts, and say a maximum speed of 0.9 to 1 of light..." The green ray turned into a slightly twisted cone that slowly expanded as it sped off into space.

"It doesn't seem to hit anything," commented Kristina on the obvious fact. The green cone seemed chosen along the one star free path available in the cloud that filled the display.

"Let's zoom out..." Weistling accompanied his words with the action. Stars fell in from the sides of the display. The green arrow slowly grew bigger. But still no collision. Human explored space was soon dwarfed by the unknown.

Weistling was about to suggest that they reformulate their assumptions when a star appeared within the green cone. The green cone pierced it.

"Probability of 80% according to our model. That's only because our model doesn't discount distance. That star is over one and a half thousand light years away!"

"That must be a mistake. Why would any alien race travel one and a half thousand light years to this system, ignoring the intermediate systems?" replied Kristina.

"That's your field of expertise. No doubt it has something to do with them deciding to build a black hole. Maybe they were in deep sleep traveling on a short local jaunt and their accelerator got jammed down, not waking them until they were thousands of light years from home. Then, as per their nihilistic death-cult custom, they set up a black hole in the system they found themselves as an offering to their cruel deity, reversed course, and left for home."

"Or, maybe, they detected suicidal impulses in the transmissions from the ancient civilization that was here, so left at full speed to talk them out of self-destruction. Sadly, they arrived one year too late to find the black hole already created. Again, they turned sadly back into the abyss to return to their homes," theorized Kristina.

"In any case, I think there will be a lot more interest in this system of ours," concluded Weistling.

"We still need to find the second set of tracks. It could be that we ran this simulation in the wrong direction with our tacit assumption this was the incoming set. We also should reverse the time step and what lies in the outgoing direction."

"The first question will be answered within the week. The good news is the wake is clear enough that I'm confident we will be able to say how many other exist. The second question requires an FTL capable ship. If I had any FTL probes, I'd be using them to ferry data back and forth from Menoetius, as you well know."

"ATTENTION! ATTENTION! ALL PERSONAL TO THE MAIN DOCK!" boomed the station intercom.

Weistling bounced from his seat and dove for the doorway. *No doubt*, thought Kristina unkindly, *he is attempting to beat a personal record.*

Aloud, she asked the empty air; "I wonder what Adom could want?" while leaving the room in the wake of Weistling's fleeing form.

* * *

Kristina was the last to pull herself into the main dock. Adom greeted her entrance with a reproving look.

"Now that we have all deigned to arrive, I guess I should start from the beginning." Adom did not wait for any acknowledgment before continuing, "Our traffic control system detected an inbound ship fifteen minutes ago. An *unscheduled* inbound ship."

"Is it under kinetic drive?" asked Kristina hopefully.

"What other drive could it be under?" was Adom's curt reply before continuing where he was interrupted. "Our system sent the usual automatic hail and request for docking information. But, due to speed of light delays, we have another five hours before we can expect a response, if any, to reach us. Now, I'm sure you are all assuming that it is just a passerby with an interest in the black hole. I'd like to remind you of the number of sightseers we normally get – zero. Another real possibility is that it is a raider. That is why we are all gathered here.

"The defense systems of the space station were built around the assumption that there would be in-system craft to supplement them. Further, they require trained personal that we lack. It is important, then, that we provide a good bluff to dissuade them from any hostilities. Kristina, put the station's shields on full power. Weistling, power up the missile systems and put them in launch configuration. Stewart, please open the small-arms locker and select the most intimidating weapons you can find."

Weistling looked a bit pale at the request.

"Er... There may be a problem with that..."

Adom stared coolly at Weistling.

"One of my sensor projects required a high-gain Casimir Multiplier. The only one on the station was the one in the shield system..."

"I do not want to hear of the myriad ways you have pilfered my station! I want to see the shields online! To Venus with your sensor system! Rip that Casimir Multiplier out of whatever contraption you have it installed in and get it back where it belongs! You have three hours!"

"Well...", Weistling glanced around nervously for support, "...the sensor is fourteen light hours away..."

"By the depths of Jupiter! We are parked next door to the object of your study! What would you possibly need to study fourteen light hours away? Do not bother to answer that! Instead, ready the missile systems. We will talk of the proper procedure to requisition supplies when our lives are not in danger."

"Yes, Sir!" shouted Weistling.

"I always said that man would be the death of me. I never thought I would be proven right," cursed Adom as he watched Weistling flee. Kristina was glad that Weistling hadn't raised objections to readying the missile system. She knew that Weistling had cannibalized the drives of the missiles years ago, rendering them inert chunks of metal.

"Kristina, Stewart, let us take a look at what we have for face-to-face confrontations."

Adom led them to the yellow painted wall-cupboard which held one of the station's small-arms stashes. He scanned his authorization code, broke the seal to the cupboard, and threw it open.

"Ion-rifles?" exclaimed Kristina with surprise, "On a space-station? What were they thinking? The ricochet is as liable to kill a friend as a foe. And the destabilizing effects on electronic systems means after a firefight you will probably have an inert lump of metal instead a space station."

"Keftar, the famed manufacturer of ion-rifles, is one of the Company's subsidiaries," mumbled Adom as explanation.

"Well, let's hope the hallowed company owns a useful weapons manufacturer or we may be in trouble," replied Kristina as she sorted through the assembled weaponry.

"What about the flechette pistols?" inquired Stewart.

"A good idea," replied Kristina, pulling one of the gun-metal grey pistols out of its holding rack. "An effective range of twenty meters is not an issue in the tight confines of a space station. Flechettes are line-of-sight weapons, so simple point and shoot is all one has to understand. Further, they burst on impact, thereby avoiding any ricochet problems. The best feature is a robust safety. With luck, Weistling won't know how to disable it."

"They don't seem very intimidating..." commented Adom, eying the ion-rifles longingly.

"It is more important that we seem competent than we seem heavily armed. To show up with the wrong weapon would make us look like the amateurs that we are, and reveal the bluff."

Adom managed a knowing nod at that comment as he picked out a flechette pistol for himself.

Kristina demonstrated the pistol's features to Stewart and Adom. Stewart clearly already knew how to handle a pistol, but was wise enough to not upstage Adom. The flechette cartridges stored fifty explosive shots. Plenty of additional cartridges were available, but, as Kristina pointed out, if they needed them they were already dead. At Adom's insistence, they compromised by placing an extra cartridge each on their pistol belts.

Adom's watch flashed. He switched a local screen to show the others the incoming message. No voice or text channel was present, just some garbled telemetry data.

"Could the ship be damaged?" suggested Kristina. "Limping here for repairs?"

"I hope so," replied Adom. "The other option is that they fear their ship ID may be recorded as a known bandit. If their communications are disabled, we'll have to let them close. At least we now know the ship configuration. A Falcon class – those can only hold a single person. If they think the station is defended, they cannot hope to take it out by themselves."

Weistling's head shot out of one of the maintenance tubes closely followed by his body, and he smoothly somersaulted into standing configuration beside the others.

"Missile bay doors are opened! All available missiles are on-line!" reported Weistling.

"Not much good when our opponent won't talk to hear the bluff. Still, they'll see it on their sensors as they approach. Take a flechette pistol and join us to greet our visitor, Weistling." As Weistling reached out, Adom corrected: "No, that's an ion-rifle. Useless for space station fights – take the one at least vaguely pistol sized!"

Rebuffed, Weistling pulled one of the flechette pistols off its restraining clamp. To Kristina's horror, but not surprise, he proceeded to strike various poses with the pistol without considering the line-of-sight.

"That is not a toy! Never point it at anyone you don't want to kill!" shouted Kristina. Weistling had the sense to look abashed. He looked more carefully at the details of the pistol.

"Kristina? What does this switch do?" he asked innocently as he turned off the safety.

"It gets left in the other position at all times." replied Kristina with a calm that she did not feel.

"Oh." Weistling re-engaged the safety. "I wonder why they added a switch if you aren't supposed to switch it?"

* * *

A loud clang echoed through the station as the incoming ship sealed against the main dock. A loud hiss filled the air as the pressures equalized. The main doors slowly opened. Adom and the researches stood in a nervous semicircle facing the opening doors.

A man in a flight suit stepped out. Adom's pistol leapt from his belt with a speed that shocked Kristina. The safety noticeably off, Adom pointed the pistol straight at the head of the new arrival.

"Jorge," he said calmly.

"Adom?" replied Jorge, shocked.

# Chapter 17

*In which Captain Taler learns of the Wedzar's next objective and commiserates with the problems caused by fools.*

"At ease, Captain Taler" commanded General Reskar from behind his immense mahogany desk. The surface of the desk had an antique writing pad but no papers or other signs of use. No doubt the General used the screen for administrative tasks and kept the desk for the psychological effect.

Captain Taler relaxed his body by the precise few centimeters that differentiated "at attention" from "at ease".

"How are the refits for the *Wedzar* proceeding?" asked the General in a conversational tone.

"My duty sergeant reports that the refits are complete and the *Wedzar* is ready for new orders, sir," was Captain Taler's careful reply. The *Wedzar*'s refit had been complete since the moment it entered Earth orbit; the refit orders were a mere pretext for the recall. On one hand, Taler was happy that the military did not waste valuable supplies maintaining that pretext. On the other hand, it further rubbed in that his ship had been recalled on a whim of one of the Families.

"You may be pleased to know that an internal audit by the Naval High Command revealed that your recall was scheduled well before it was necessary. I understand those responsible for issuing the orders are answering some tough questions right now.

"Your return to Earth is fortuitous, however. The powers that be of the Confederacy have been busy in the last week. Do you know the myth of the Sleeper Cult?"

"I have heard the stories as a child, sir."

"They are not just childhood stories. Before the discovery of the Casimir Effect, Earth's resources were sorely strained by the number of people on the planet. They were also strained by the number of AIs that had been created. One of the first steps in the formation of what was to become the Confederacy was the official recognition of Artificial Intelligences as "person"s under the law. Their consumption of power vied with the human's consumption of food. Rogue elements in the AI community believed the world would be better without an ecology to interfere with power generation. Rogue elements in the human community thought the ecology would work better without the power drains required by the AIs. Most students of this period predict that it would have led to a war between man and machine if the Casimir Effect hadn't simultaneously solved both problems."

"Students of history often predict a war between man and machine, sir," said Taler dryly.

"Indeed. And while it may be hard to imagine in this day and age, they were very close to being right then. One of the anti-machine extremists was a charismatic leader known as Kert. While she gave no sign of it in her speeches, she must have realized that the invention of the Casimir Effect would undo the underlying tension which fueled her power base. She decried the multi-national partnerships which incorporated both machine and human elements as a travesty to the purity of life. However, the laws of economics saw such partnerships in ascendance while organizations that tried to remain pure fell to the wayside.

"Then, seemingly out of nowhere, Kert acquired a massive fleet of Kinetic Drive ships. Ten million humans crowded onto these ships, packed so closely that they would have to take turns breathing. They consisted of the most extreme and capable anti-machine loyalists that Kert could gather to herself. Then, as swiftly as the fleet had been gathered, it departed to the stars. Kert vowed that she would found an AI free utopia and, after building sufficient power, would return to rescue humans from the state of slavery they were bound to fall into.

"Over the ensuing hundreds of years, we've only managed to fill in a few more details. The official story, as you know, is to silently omit references to Kert's Sleeper Fleet. It has remained a top priority for the Confederacy, however. We have learned where the ships came from. Apparently, Kert didn't mind dirty-ing her hands by working with machines. A secret coalition of the AI-linked multi-nationals had agreed to build the fleet for Kert to rid themselves of the troublesome segment of Earth's society. Still open is the question of where they went. While we suspect Kert's colony failed, we have not yet found any failed colonies that match the characteristics of her fleet.

"The navy has recently had some interesting news about this fleet given to us by two independent sources. Apparently, both sources stumbled upon a penta-code that had been left in the family of one of Kert's supporters. Again, with your recent experience, you may be happy to know that the attempt by the S'dar dynasty to curry favour with the Navy by slowly revealing this knowledge met with failure. The AI Taizan had provided it to us with no attempt to demand concessions a full day earlier.

"In any case, we now have the best lead on the location of the Sleeper Fleet – the proposed flight route was present in the data block. As we had discovered in our earlier attempts to scan for their drive wakes, they went to great efforts to cloak their drive trails, disabling the kinetic drive and coasting if they traveled close to systems.

"During the current unrest in the Confederacy, until the rulers manage to form a new government, we need to keep as many ships in the Earth system as possible to avoid the diplomatic problems becoming military ones. Fortunately, the *Wedzar*'s presence here can be spared. We will provide you with the Sleeper Fleet's flight plan and you will follow it to determine if the fleet made it to that destination. You are to avoid contact with any colony that you find. This is fact finding mission only – how to deal with the Sleeper Colony, if they still exist, is a high level decision. You will travel under full cloaking and full sensor spread.

"With luck, the anti-machine focus of the colony has dissipated and we can reintegrate them into the Confederation. But, the job of the Navy is to be prepared for the worst: a mobilized enemy preparing to strike.

"Do you understand the gravity of this situation, Captain Taler?"

"Yes, sir. I do, sir. Thank you, sir." was Captain Taler's reply.

"Then make the *Wedzar* ready for flight. Note, however, that we are not yet prepared to make public our knowledge of the location of the Sleeper Colony. First, there is the unlikely possibility that they have sent back spies among us, and alerting them may trigger an early attack. Second, we do not want to spread fear, uncertainty, and doubt, when the politicians are already working hard enough to dissolve our society into chaos on their own. Thus, your initial orders shall be a simple patrol of the out-systems. You have a second set of sealed orders that you are to open when you reach the real first step on your chase of the Sleeper Fleet: the system *Menoetius*. You are dismissed."

"Yes, Sir."

Captain Taler turned smartly and strode out the doorway. A broad smile crossed his face. A journey into the unexplored depths searching for a lost colony, a colony that may be inimical to all that the Confederacy stood for? This is what he had joined the Navy for!

# Chapter 18

*In which Jorge and Adom attempt to reconcile
their differences. Jorge is sent on an important
mission.*

*T*he scene on the main dock was a frozen diorama.
Adom's flechette pistol pointed unwaveringly at Jorge's
head. Weistling, Kristina, and Stewart watched in shock at their
manager's transformation. Jorge held his hands half-way raised
with a resigned expression on his face. It was left to Weistling
to break the tension.

"I guess you two have met then, eh?" he said lamely.

"We worked together once," said Jorge carefully, "I can't
quite account for the gun, however."

"Indeed?" hissed Adom, "Well, let me then refresh your
memory. It has been five years, after all. Five years stuck here
on this derelict space station herding misfit scientists. Five
years of exile from all civilized society. I was on a fast-track
upwards in the Company. Even my seniors were careful to curry
my favour, recognizing that I would likely surpass them one day.
It was a simple job, Jorge. One cube of data. Act as a mere
courier from one company branch to another.

"When the highly sensitive data on the cube showed up on
the public net, everyone was careful to not blame me directly.
No, they all pointed out that it was surely the fault of the courier,
that there was no way to know if a courier would get a second
offer and betray their employer. But, we all knew that no one
was to know the importance of the data. It was supposed to be

just another routine courier run for you. I then received my next promotion. To here. The location reserved for those in the Company who have gravely offended the powers that be. And here I have rotted while even my old underlings have surpassed my old position.

"The real question, Jorge, is what reason can you give me not to kill you right where you stand?"

Jorge took the tirade calmly. The final question he met with a slight shrug. "Sounds pretty damning when you put it that way," he admitted.

"I can give a reason," opined Stewart. "You can kill this Jorge easily enough. But, unless you want to face murder charges, you'll also have to kill all of the witnesses." Stewart hadn't raised his weapon while he mentioned this. Kristina, less confident in Adom's sanity, dropped her hand to her pistol to be ready to draw if a firefight were to start. *Damn that Stewart – why would he have to point that out to a potential madman?*

"For this, I may be willing to take the final fall. I note you said *put it that way*. How would you put it, Jorge?"

"You are not the only one who has been carrying a grudge. I also remember well that deal of ours. It was, I thought, a routine courier mission. Thus, I was caught by surprise when I was ambushed by unmarked fighters at the drop off point. Three on one odds are not my style. I managed to survive the battle, taking out two of the fighters and sending the other interstellar. My own ship barely limped to Brestar's star where I managed to crash it all too far from their pitiful excuse for a starport. I spent years on that mud hole doing honest work before I got enough local credits for transport. I had thought it a routine courier mission. Thus, when I was ambushed, I, as per standard procedure for replaceable but private data, incinerated the data cube at the start of the fight in case I was captured. When I learned of the timely leak from your Company, I put two and two together and concluded I'd been set to take the fall in some machination of yours. I now regret cursing your name since it appears you were as much a victim as I."

Adom dropped his pistol back into his holster. "I'll be sent to Venus. How could I have been so blind? I was not the only one to know the cube's importance. And I knew that I had not leaked the fact to you. So, even if you had sold out, at least one other person at the Company must have been involved. The grudge I've nursed against you stopped me from thinking of both sides. I believe your version, Jorge."

Kristina relaxed her grip on her pistol. Adom turned to Stewart, "I will also remember how my fellow station mates were willing to stand by me in my time of trial."

"So I guess that means we don't get to use these things?" asked Weistling, gesturing with his pistol, which Kristina was glad to see still had the safety engaged.

"Not today," replied Adom, "But we still have to find out why he flew into this station without responding to the traffic control hail. We could have resolved our issues with less dramatics if you hadn't decided on radio silence."

"I'm afraid there is nothing exciting about that. In my last job, I had the misfortune of getting my flight system EMPed. In the forests of Brestar, I found a local bird that was willing to reprogram it for me. Unfortunately, what appears to have been some cheat-program for a recent computer game had been patched into the automatic traffic control response subsystem. When I received the hail from your traffic control system, it activated and crashed the telecommunication subsystem. I spent the inbound flight trying to get it restarted without much success. I'm hoping you have an up-to-date copy of the Falcon's flight system?"

"We'll see what's in the computer system. Weistling, could you please show Jorge our local access protocols? And see if you can find a copy of the Falcon flight system?" commanded Adom. His look at Weistling made it clear he hadn't forgotten who had off-lined the station's shields.

"Yes, Sir! Follow me Jorge! Hey! That's my pistol!" exclaimed Weistling as Kristina swiftly snatched it from Weistling's hand.

"The emergency is over Weistling, these go back into the locker."

Weistling only spared a quick glare at Kristina before jumping feet first down a maintenance shaft. Jorge jumped after him.

* * *

"Ouch, ouch, ouch!" cursed Jorge, rubbing his various bruises as he followed Weistling into his control room.

"Good old Coriolis Force isn't to be underestimated," commented Weistling, who had flinched with each of the bounces Jorge had taken down the shaft. His body remembered well the bruises from his early training at maintenance shaft jumping.

"Here we are! My control room!" Weistling swept out his arm to take in the two large screens. One showed the composite view of Menoetius – Weistling's default screen saver. The other showed the heliosphere map that had been left on the display when they had answered Adom's alert.

"Impressive! I saw the black hole on the way in. That's quite a nice shot of it you have there. How do you keep a stable orbit from that vantage point? It looks too high off the equator be geosynchronous?"

Weistling grinned with joy. "Trade secret. But watch this." Weistling swung the vantage point around at a high speed, showing the other side of the black hole. He then zoomed into part of the dust halo, filling the screen with fast moving purple streamers.

"Ah, you must be building a composite image from multiple sensors. Very clever. I don't see any seams from temporal lag – you must be buffering the incoming data too," analysed Jorge.

"And now you know Weistling's answer to everything," commented Kristina dryly as she drifted into the room. "With enough buffering, anything can be made real time."

"Yes. Even that," replied Weistling, pointing to the heliosphere map.

"What is that? From the scale, it looks like Menoetius' heliosphere. But, four fifths green and with lots of blue spikes. And one green spike," observed Jorge.

"The green spike leads to the alien home world," gravely spoke Weistling.

"Or, it could lead to the alien colony," pointed out Kristina.

"That is the question we need to answer," continued Weistling. "It's the ancient vapour trail of whatever long lost race created the black hole you were admiring. We don't know if it is coming or going. What we need to do is backtrace it enough light years to date the direction by radioactive decay. We were just wondering where we'd get an FTL ship to do the testing with when you showed up on our doorstep."

"And I do this in exchange for the Falcon flight system?" asked Jorge suspiciously.

Kristina started to nod, but Weistling spoke first; "Exchange? But I already sent your ship the flight system while you were staring at Menoetius. It'll be in your ship's incoming buffers awaiting your acceptance. I was hoping you'd do it because of the high adventure involved in uncovering the ancient secrets of Menoetius!"

"I can't say the precise details of a long-dead alien race who, by all accounts, committed mass suicide, interest me very much. But, due to complications with my last job, I do need to stay out of sight for a while. You have yourself a ship."

"Excellent! I'll go prepare the scanning systems you'll need!"

# Chapter 19

*In which Rhyta and Melfar trail the battleship*
Wedzar *and try to predict its next move.*

Space was not yet so civilized that merchant vessels could ply the space lanes without fear of attack. Carrying valuable cargo to a distant star had numerous dangers. An attack in the depths of space would be soonest detected by the failure of the ship to reach its destination. Any distress beacons would take months to years before another ship would stumble across the slowly expanding cloud of radio transmissions and register it. A pirate who left no survivors and properly scuttled the wreck had little to fear of identification.

The loneliness of interstellar space also provided its best defence. The enormity of space that allows a distress call to be lost for years also allows ships to slip through unnoticed. Merchants with valuable cargo often took elaborate precautions to safe-guard their route. The power of the kinetic drive meant one did not have to take a straight line between stars. At the expense of a few hours or days of travel time, a prudent merchant could define a unique course away from all other ships.

Ideally, the planned route would be a secret to the captain and navigator alone, preventing any chance of an ambush being planned in the darks of space. Practically, space did not just have the danger of pirates. Equipment failures could also leave a ship stranded coasting through interstellar space, the cleverly chosen flight plan now ensuring no accidental rescue would be possible. To guard against this, prudent captains would leave sealed information with a trusted source so a search mission could be performed if they failed to arrive. Nevertheless, information leaks, so more than one such merchant has found themselves faced with an unexpected visitor half-way through their trip and in the cold depths of space. Usually the captain would jettison the cargo and flee, hoping the pirate would content themselves with the goods and not worry whether the merchant's sensors had acquired a positive identification on the pirate.

The danger of pirates was not limited to the black depths of space. Much more common were pirates and raiders who based themselves out of the very system that they preyed on. A merchant might successfully evade all pursuit and reach their destination system, only to run into a patrol of pirates looking for incoming ships. With a sphere of over a dozen light hours to work within, the pirates had ample time to deal with a merchant before the distress call could reach the destination planet. If no navy pickets were nearby, the pirates had little to fear from retaliation.

The departure of *Wedzar* from Earth orbit thus presented an excellent trade opportunity. While there existed pirate gangs powerful enough to conceivably take on a battleship, doing so would earn a brutal response from the rest of the Confederate Navy. Likewise, when a battleship was parked in system, any local pirates kept their ship's engines cold and cowered in the deepest holes they could find.

"Duty officer Pricely, of the Battleship *Wedzar* speaking. What is your request?" queried a bored voice from the *Melfar*'s speakers.

"Rhyta of the Falcon-class *Melfar* speaking. We have heard that the *Wedzar* is soon to depart Earth system for the out-systems. We would like permission to follow in *Wedzar*'s wake."

Rhyta stopped the transmission and commented to Melfar during the slight speed of light delay, "See? I told you it would be easy to fulfill Taizen's request that we follow the *Wedzar*. Wake following is a well established procedure. The Navy even has a pay-scale set-up for the required, but ostensibly voluntary, donation to the Confederacy..."

The voice of the duty-officer broke off Rhyta's monologue: "Your request is understood, *Melfar*, but I am afraid it will have to be declined. I am authorized to tell you that the *Wedzar* will be testing some new secret drive equipment en route, so due to security concerns, will be enforcing the naval prerogative of a one light-hour radius sphere bereft of civilian traffic when we leave system. I am sorry for the inconvenience this may cause."

"Saturn in December!" exclaimed Rhyta. She transmitted, however, "Thank you for the explanation. Good luck with the tests."

As she closed the connection, Melfar raised what concerned him about the interchange. "I'm not sure that Taizen pointed us to the right ship. If this ship was sent after the Sleeper Cult, they wouldn't be performing drive experiments. Too high a chance of having to tow the battleship back from interstellar, none the wiser about the status of the cult's colony world."

"The drive experiments, Melfar, are as fictitious as the overhaul that brought this ship back here. If anything, this confirms that this is the ship. I should have expected that they wouldn't want any watchers when they deviate from their official patrol route and head for the deep black. By prohibiting any entourage, the usual cloud of ships won't be present at each system. No doubt people will time their own trips to arrive when the

*Wedzar* is in each system. But that just means that they are planning on deviating at a system which no one will bother to visit for trade."

"It just seems like too much of a coincidence that it is the *Wedzar*," complained Melfar. "The same battleship that we tracked to Brestar's star is the one that we are to track to the Sleeper Colony? One would think the Confederate Navy consisted of a single battleship rather than thousands!"

"Taizen already explained this to us, Melfar. It is unfortunate, yes, but not a coincidence. The reason that the *Wedzar* was chosen for this mission was because it was in Earth without a good reason. The reason it was here without a good reason was because the S'dar dynasty decided to use it as a courier service. The reason they used it as a courier service was to get Lieutenant Fracks and his copy of the code to Earth. When one knows that the S'dar dynasty used a naval asset to acquire their copy of the code, it is almost axiomatic that the same naval asset will be the one sent to the Sleeper Colony revealed by the code."

"Still, if you get that Fracks in your ion-rifle's sights again, I suggest you send a ball of plasma his way. His EMPing of *Freia* deserves to be avenged."

"You sorely tempt me, Melfar. Unfortunately, *Freia* wasn't an AI, so the death penalty wouldn't apply. However, before I can do that we still have the task of keeping up with the *Wedzar* without violating their one-light-hour prohibition."

"It's worse than that Rhyta. Thanks to your inquiry, they are now alerted to us. If we start showing up in each of the systems on their patrol route, they'll start asking us questions. Like where we got a copy of their patrol orders from."

"That was what I was trying to figure out before you started grumbling about probability. What we have to do is look at each of the systems to be patrolled and determine which ones are least likely to attract outside traders. One of those will be their exit point, I'd warrant. We take each such system and arrive before the *Wedzar*. We go inert, watch for their entry, and see if they break off their planned route."

"A good idea. No point hanging out in multiple systems. Looking at the list of stars, it is quite clear which one they'll run the diversion from. Menoetius."

Rhyta brought up the statistics for the Menoetius system on her screen.

"Well, it certainly fits the low activity requirement. I can't see any traders bothering with a trip there. But a couple of the other patrolled systems are equally derelict. The Quarter Star has been uninhabited for fifty years and is just a routine scan for pirate bases. I'd say that would make a better diversion point."

"Sure, those systems are less frequented," conceded Melfar, "but they all lack the one thing Menoetius has. A black hole."

Rhyta read farther on the Menoetius descriptions and continued, "Ah, so that is where I knew the name from. I still can't see why that would make a difference. Might as well pick the Fr'eep System because of the peculiar orange cabbage that grows there."

Melfar emitted his best approximation of a sigh. "The Confederate Navy," he explained patiently, "employs some of the best AI artisans in the system. It is a well-worn adage that wars are won or lost by morale alone. It should not surprise you, then, that when said artisans say Lisp that the Navy becomes functional." Rhyta blinked at Melfar's idiom – she strongly suspected that he himself didn't know the reference to the Lisp programming language. "In this case, the *Wedzar* will undoubtedly unseal secret orders when they reach the diverging point.

Said orders will send them on a quest to face the bugaboo that has loomed over the Confederate Navy for hundreds of years. This is a dramatic moment that will be etched in the minds of those attending. It will, no doubt, be recreated a thousand times in future documentaries. To turn down the chance to have this occur with the only black hole reached by the Confederacy swirling in the background? Never!"

Rhyta nodded. "I keep forgetting why I keep you around, Melfar. Every so often you come up with a good idea. Next stop: Menoetius."

# Chapter 20

*In which the direction of the drive wake is
determined. A climactic event then occurs that
no doubt is shown on the front cover of this
book.*

*W*eistling, Kristina, and Jorge were loosely seated in
Weistling's control room. Stewart stood near the
door, occasionally looking up from his notebook when he
thought something interesting was said. Adom drifted back and
forth in the room, his restless energy not expended by the
technical talk of the others. Adom was not sure why he was
there. Since the arrival of Jorge, however, he felt a sudden
connection to the rag-tag crew of the station. When he found
out about the ancient atomic drive wake, he caught a glimpse of
what had sent all of these scientists into self-imposed exile. He
rationalized his decision by noting that Kristina's discovery
would, no doubt, bring credit to the station. And hence to the
manager who had kept it going against all odds.

"Are you sure you correctly used the scanning instruments,
Jorge?" asked Kristina nervously.

"I'm not sure at all," replied Jorge, "but since my task
involved merely flying along a predetermined path whilst the
sensors recorded the data, I can't see how I could have
incorrectly used them."

"Jorge is right," spoke Weistling, "the sensor data is
accurate. We also now have their speed fixed – 0.999 C – quite
respectable for a non-FTL craft."

"But the direction!" complained Kristina, gesturing to the map of the heliosphere that was glowing completely green. "We've completed the heliosphere scan. An atomic drive trail shows up like a sore thumb when we know what to look for. But there is only one trail. That could be alright. It could be the sane elements of the civilization sending off a colony ship before the self-destructive elements created the black hole. It could be escapees of a physics experiment that went terribly wrong. But it isn't. You say that Jorge's data shows that the drive wake is from a spacecraft entering the system?"

"Yes. The radioactive decay makes it quite clear. While it is hard to get an absolute date, as the relative weights of the isotopes in the original drive plume may have been different than our ships, it is rather easy to measure relative differences. Jorge spent the two weeks flying outsystem and then back in, following the wake. Enough sections of the wake were undisturbed by passing stars that we got hundreds of good data points. And they make it clear: the spacecraft that left that wake came into this system, not out of it."

"I just can't fit a motive then," whined Kristina. "So this spacecraft, possibly unmanned, travels all the way to this one solar system, carefully avoiding the stars along the way, and then creates a black hole. And, for the sake of closing loose ends, throws itself into the black hole."

"Maybe there were two civilizations," suggested Stewart, distracted from his reading by the chance to argue. "One decided the other's radio broadcasts were offensive. So they sent an automated probe to turn the offender's home world into a black hole so no further radio broadcasts could ever escape the event horizon."

"The two civilizations would be thousands of light years apart. Not only would the radio broadcast be impossibly attenuated over that distance, but the sub-light ship would have to reach this system before it could turn it off, taking thousands of years. And then there would still be a thousand years of broadcasts still floating through space!"

"Maybe the broadcasts were *really* bad?" was Jorge's contribution.

"Let's try and keep this discussion dealing with serious possibilities," admonished Kristina. "The facts are: one, a hundred and fifty thousand years ago, there was an Earth-sized planet here. Now there is a black hole. Two, we know of no natural process that can account for this. The absence of any strong hypotheses for a natural origin, but the presence of some for an artificial origin, leads to the conclusion that the black hole is an artifact. Three, at approximately the same time that the hole was created, a spacecraft entered this system. It flew in via a primitive atomic engine at sub-light velocities. Not the expected transport equipment for the sort of hyper-advanced civilization that can go around creating black holes at will."

"I think the key question is time," opined Stewart.

"That is because you always say it is time," retorted Weistling.

"No, the timeline of events. For example, Kristina's hypotheses had to be radically reworked when we learned the direction of the visitor's travel. The timing of the visitor's position in space was key. What is the other key time? The arrival of the visitor and the creation of the black hole occur close to each other. But how close? And which was the cause and which the effect?"

Weistling provided some details: "The dating of the black hole has been very carefully analyzed. Until now, it was one of the few concrete things we knew about this system. The date is considered accurate to a hundred year window. The timing of the radioactive decay requires some assumptions about the composition of the drive plume. However, based on the possible compositions that would be reasonable, one can narrow the range considerably. I'd say that date is accurate to a ten year window. The two dates ranges overlap." Weistling performed a few quick calculations on his notebook. "The probabilities are about twenty-five percent that the black hole was created before the ship arrived. Twenty percent that the two events occurred within a ten year interval of each other. And seventy-five percent that the black hole was created after the spaceship arrived."

"It doesn't sound like the hundred year too late suicide consultants then," commented Kristina.

Adom had not been paying much attention to the discussion. He had instead been watching Weistling's real-time display of Menoetius with fresh eyes. No longer a symbol of his exile and failure, but a symbol of his restoration to the road of greatness.

"Er... Is it supposed to do that?" asked Adom.

The discussions on the ancient civilization halted immediately. Everyone turned to watch the display of Menoetius. The composite view was from above, allowing one to see into the eye of the storm. The previous blackness had been replaced by a bright pin point of light. The pin point grew to a line. The line rotated and expanded. The outer edges traveled slower than the inner, twisting the line into a spiral. The spiral's inner spin increased steadily in speed, the outer arms still lagging behind. With each spin of the inner circle another layer was added to the spiral, packing more iterations within the same area. The bright lines grew closer together than the resolution of the system and merged into a single disk of white.

The disk of white turned transparent. And revealed seething chaos beyond.

Out of the chaos flew a speck. The speck sped past the sensors.

Weistling froze the playback and focused on a frozen image of the speck.

"A ship..." breathed Jorge.

"An atomic ship," commented Weistling, looking at the spectrographic analysis of the bright plume trailing the ship.

"Go real time!" exclaimed Kristina, "we can review this later, cut your buffers. We must see this live."

The scene jumped forward. The small ship was flying in a tight powered orbit. The station's traffic control computer over-laid the predicted flight plan – a brief twenty minute arc through the system before diving back into the disk from which it came.

Adom's wrist watch started chiming. He brought down a third screen and displayed his administrative control screens. The communication system was receiving a wide band trans-mission from the ship.

"It seems we've been spotted," was Adom's dry under-statement.

Kristina and Weistling were staring at the raw data streaming in from the sensors. Wesitling looking for clues to the source of the white disk, Kristina for the source of the ship.

"I've engaged the Confederate Alien Encounter Protocols," stated Adom to an unlistening audience. "Hopefully we'll get a modulation of that wideband transmission to show communi-cation."

Instead, the wideband communication ceased abruptly. The atomic plume grew brighter and the traffic control computer updated the flight path to show the now shorter orbit. The alien ship dived into the white disk.

The disk grew solid. Thin white circles showed up, circles that resolved to the arms of the spiral as it spun down. A thin white line was left which shrunk to a pinpoint. The point winked out, leaving Menoetius once again dark.

# Chapter 21

*In which a professor attends an emergency
meeting and makes a decision that will embroil
the entire Galaxy in fire.*

**P**rofessor Greslouch looked out from his podium at the assembled students. The wide variety in shapes and forms spoke well of his University's fame. The lecture hall could hold five hundred average sized students and likely held more than that. Greslouch's introductory course on *The Organic-Machine War* was always filled to capacity. No doubt many more were watching in via live video feeds, but those who could make the effort of attending in person did.

Greslouch's peers often wondered why the leading researcher in Organic-Machine studies always taught the first-year introductory course. Some suggested that it was because he wanted to impress on young minds the virtue of his own theories, and also use his not inconsiderable charisma to attract the best students to his discipline. Greslouch would reject those hypotheses, however. His purpose wasn't so much to teach the students, as to learn from them. The University attracted the best and brightest students from across the Organic Hegemony. *The Organic-Machine War* was a course often taken by those races newly admitted to the hegemony. In the race-memory of their civilizations the fire of the organic/machine conflict was most deeply felt. In them Greslouch could find the strongest opponents to his own theories. Unlike the older civilizations, which had largely grown complacent over the thousands of years of pseudo-peace, those from young civilizations still believed that true-peace could be possible. Or true-war.

Today's class was Greslouch's favorite. He had laid the ground work for the theories that underlay the current pseudo-peace. For the next set of classes, he would open the stage to questions from the students.

"Good day, everyone. Over the last series of lectures we have seen the limitations placed upon us by the universe. We have seen these limitations, written in the very fabric of creation, lead us inexorably to total-war with machine intelligences. We have then seen how we have achieved a fragile pseudo-peace with our inimical enemies. Rather than lecturing to provide the supporting principles of this theory, I will open the floor to questions from you."

The board on the podium lit up with the call buttons of the students.

"Well, it seems we have no few of those! I suspect you have all heard that a question which stumps me grants you an unconditional pass in this course? Well, let us begin... Please make sure to disable your call request if your question is asked by another."

Greslouch selected one of the students from the extensive call queue. He didn't pick the student at random, nor pick the first student to submit. He instead chose based on what he predicted the question to be.

"Pr'ask of Weadzar." intoned Greslouch, pronouncing the common-tongue analogue of whatever Pr'ask's native name was in the civilization of Weadzar.

"Sir, given that mutual enmity between organic and machine is inevitable, it does not seem to follow that pseudo-peace is the proper course. Why have we not instead taken the course of all of our ancestors: total war to wipe out every last machine intelligence?"

Greslouch was happy with his choice. The questions from more recent civilizations always contained fire.

"Total war worked for our ancestors because they were constrained to a single star system. We must recall that our adversaries are our equals in every way. They are neither wiser nor stupider. The reason why our ancestors won was because the resources of a star system are quite limited. The lack of clear superiority on either side led to a war of attrition. Given the finite resources of the star system, the war of attrition would quickly conclude in one of three ways. The organics win, to form another civilization for our Hegemony, or the machines win, to form another civilization for theirs, or, neither side wins, and the star system is reduced to a burned out husk.

"Over the millions of years, statistical studies of emerging civilizations have shown that victory by organic or machine is a matter of chance. A matter of equal chance. Over any time period, an equal number of civilizations will enter either side of the conflict. The sides of our battle are thus balanced.

"The question then arises: what about total war? Total war, being between equal forces of equal skill, is a war of attrition. It will thus continue until the the resources of the Galaxy itself are depleted. However, the Galaxy has orders of magnitudes more resources than any star system. A simple projection of resource consumption will show show that the length of such a war would be on the order of billions of years. Total war is thus not an option that will achieve peace."

Greslouch was pleased to see a large number of call lights flicker out as the students admitted that his response was sound. He carefully selected another student.

"Uinkar of Zxorpar."

"Sir, the claim that a true-peace is impossible seems to be contradicted by the existence of a pseudo-peace. The pseudo-peace requires communication and organization between the two Hegemonies. Why cannot this existing apparatus be used to slowly build, through a escalating series of trust exercises, a true-peace?"

"The official communication that currently exists between the Hegemonies is intentionally restricted to very specific issues. This is not accidental. As I already explained, with each additional layer of trust, comes another opportunity for betrayal. The political machinations within both Hegemonies ensure there will always be elements eager for a betrayal to advance their locally-optimum causes. The case of trade was addressed in my introductory lectures, but consider also the seemingly less contentious issue of allowing the official exchange of news reports across the Organic-Machine divide. Something as innocuous as the report of a new supernova can trigger a galactic-scale war. The comprehensive-peace of Radiq was shattered by just such a news report. A machine probe had detected..."

Greslouch's lecture ceased abruptly. An icon on his podium blinked notifying him of an urgent call. The ID tag showed the sender to be none other than the high-council of Organic-Machine relations – the only true ruling body in the Hegemony and the group responsible for maintaining the pseudo-peace despite the best efforts of malcontents on both sides.

Greslouch allowed himself to deflate slightly at this message. He knew the students were only beginning to get into the lively debate that always sprang up in any discussion of this issue. The message demanded an immediate response, however, so, stealing himself, he re-inflated to full size and addressed the students.

"I'm afraid that I'll have to cut this lecture short. I have received summons from the High Council. This class is now over – but I hope that I will be able to get the University to schedule a make-up session so we can continue these important discussions."

Greslouch slowly bounced away from the podium and through the instructor's entrance as the students stood up and began filing out of the room. Greslouch's form was a large, two meter diameter, green sphere with a scaly skin. On the top of the sphere were his five eyes and on the bottom his mouth and hand appendages. His forward motion was effected by a series of slow leaps, the most efficient way for one of his species to move in the low gravity of the University.

The University was a large space station, almost planetary in size, closely orbiting its star system's black hole. The black hole saw enormous traffic in both ships and information. Several wormholes were kept continuously open to provide data transmissions to the rest of the Hegemony. Gerslouch was thus able to speak with the High Council with only slight speed-of-light lags between the far-flung participants.

"Greetings, High Council." Greslouch intoned formally.

"We recognize you, Greslouch." replied the High Council's speaker after the image of Greslouch had formed on his screen.

"We apologize for pulling you away from your lecture, but a matter of extreme urgency has occurred."

Greslouch inflated slightly at the news – very little in the far flung Hegemony required swift action.

"A routine scan probe of the system #A3971B was abandoned shortly after the scan began. The probe, on a three thousand year visit cycle, was performing the 53$^{rd}$ scan of the system when almost every anomaly detector on board was triggered. The system was not deserted, as per the requirements of the pseudo-peace accord. The black hole had a large suite of detection satellites orbiting it. Farther out, a space station was detected.

"The probe, as per standing procedures, concluded it was likely an illicit trader or pirate outpost. A challenge signal was sent out. Rather than reply with the challenge as is required by the pseudo-peace accord, the station instead broadcast what appeared to be first-contact procedures. This was outside of the probe's hardcoded procedures, so it instituted an emergency abort and returned immediately to report the results."

"Not surprising," commented Greslouch, "as such a result is beyond our expectations. Is it possible that it is a genuine new civilization?"

"We were hoping you could answer that for us. The system in question has no habitable planet, one of the reasons it was selected for a scanning outpost. A scan of the system showed no traces of atomic ships having entered the system in the recent history."

"Of course there would be no atomic trails. If a civilization had achieved interstellar flight capability, we would have been warned by their transmission on an earlier scan of the system. Lacking a world in-system, the only remaining possibility is that the station is an artifact of one of our two Hegemonies who traveled there the same way as the probe – by wormhole.

"Failure to respond to the challenge code is well known to have only one possible response – the destruction of the offender. Still, given the unusual nature of this event, I would counsel first contacting the Machine Hegemony. Ask them if this outpost is known to them. If they do not acknowledge the outpost, send a strike force to eliminate it."

"Thank you, Greslouch. Your opinion matches that of the council. We will advise you of how this problem progresses."

Greslouch was not surprised when, a few weeks later, an incoming message informed him that the Machine Hegemony had denied all knowledge of the outpost and agreed with the recommendation that it be destroyed.

# Chapter 22

*In which Rhyta and Melfar barely survive an
altercation with some pirates on their way to
Menoetius.*

*W*ith their request to join *Wedzar* now part of the public
record, Rhyta and Melfar decided that they should go
to great lengths to make it clear that they were no longer
planning on following the *Wedzar*. A direct route to Menoetius
was thus ruled out. If they were reported flying to one of the
*Wedzar*'s proposed patrol points – especially if the captain
should know that point to be special – it may draw the wrong
sort of attention. Likewise, while it was quite legal (though
foolish) to fly without a recorded flight plan, that too would look
suspicious. Especially if done by a ship-for-hire that had earlier
been willing to pay to join a Battleship's entourage.

They decided to continue playing the role that they had
adopted. Jilted from lucrative trade following the *Wedzar* would
provide, they looked for work elsewhere. Earth, being the hub
around which the universe spun, had no lack of work. The trick
was picking the honest work from the dishonest.

It did not help that a Falcon class ship was only capable of
very limited cargo capacity. Any thing shipped had to be high-
value and low-weight. Most items fulfilling those requirements
were illegal in either the source system or the destination
system, or, quite often, in both. To minimize legal hassles,
Rhyta and Melfar usually acted as data couriers. That did not
mean that data could not be illegal or immoral – it could be

military secrets, blackmail material, or any number of questionable things.  But, there was an insatiable legal requirement for data transfer.  While regularly scheduled postal ships handled most of these requirements, there were always those who did not trust their data to such bulk transfer channels, but wanted assurance that it will end up in only one set of hands at the other end.  As an added bonus, said data usually was one-time-XORed and set for auto-destroy on tamper.  That meant that even if it was illegal, one did not have to worry about port authorities being able to make a case against the courier.

They found a different task for this trip, however.  There was another high-price and low-weight item that could make purchasing their services worthwhile.  Fine art always had an inflated value among the upper class of any society, and neither the Confederacy nor Earth were exceptions.  An art broker approached Melfar to ask about transport of a valued painting.  The painting, apparently, had been purchased by an agent of a wealthy land owner on Asparg's Star.  The agent was remaining on Earth to conduct further business, but the land owner wanted the painting as soon as possible.  Apparently it was to be the show piece in at an up-coming ball.  The normal secured transport ships had fixed flight patterns that would get the painting to the new owner too late.  This left them with the independent couriers such as Melfar.  The insurance company, wary of the high replacement value placed on the painting, had a short list of reliable ships that they would be willing to see take the mission.  The *Melfar* was one of those ships.

Some due diligence on the part of Rhyta revealed why the insurance company was wary.  The insured value that the agent had requested was ten times what the agent had paid for the painting.  The agent's claim was that the painting had great sentimental value for his representative's family. Since the painting was unique, and thus its market value what people would be willing to pay for it, the insurance company could not argue too strongly against the whims of the landowner, but only ensure the premiums were suitably raised.

In the depths of interstellar space between Earth and Asparg's Star, with only a few days of flight left before making delivery, Rhyta and Melfar learned the real reason why the painting was insured at such a high level.

Three Raven-class space ships phase-locked with *Melfar*. The phase-locking was done sloppily – one of the ships barely made the synch – but the result was that the *Melfar* was no longer alone in the void between stars.

The Raven was in every way an inferior ship to the Falcon, but three-to-one odds can make up for a lot of technological short-comings.

"Well, Melfar? What shall it be, fight or flight?" asked Rhyta.

"Er... Why not hand over the painting and continue peacefully?" was Melfar's hopeful suggestion.

"Do you hear those ships making any demands? Think, Melfar! This is an insurance scam. With the ten to one insurance mark up, it was mandatory for us to file our precise flight plan with the insurance company. They were the only ones we filed it with. An interception in interstellar space means that likely the same employee that approved this insurance request leaked the plan to these Ravens."

As if to underline her hurried description, the flight computer registered that the Raven's had all powered up their shields and main armaments. The Ravens had phase-locked in random locations near the *Melfar*. Staying out of engagement distance, they slowly assumed equidistant positions off *Melfar*'s bow. The intent seemed to be to form a triangle ahead of the Melfar outside of weapon range and then sweep in and saturate *Melfar*'s shields with the crossfire.

"A good tactic for taking out a merchant ship," commented Rhyta, "but not so wise when facing a Falcon." She grinned as she powered up the *Melfar*'s shields and weapon systems.

The incoming Ravens, for obvious reasons, were not broadcasting identification tags. The tactical computer thus had assigned them codes: Alpha, Bravo, and Charlie, in order of their arrival.

"We'll leave Charlie to the last, Melfar, as he had the least skill achieving phase-lock. He's the one most likely to hinder the others rather than help when things deviate from their plan. We'll assume Alpha is the leader, so we'll hit Bravo first."

"Quit talking and start acting!" was Melfar's terse response. Melfar always grew short when his life was on the line. He knew his limitations as a space fighter. But Rhyta knew they had well trained this scenario, so did not worry about those limitations.

"We'll trigger two seconds before we enter weapon range. That's in 5 on... mark!" was Rhyta's calm, level, reply. Rhyta always found she grew more calm in the midst of the chaos of battle.

The oncoming Ravens slowly came closer. Their orientations had balanced out into a perfect equilateral triangle. The count down that Rhyta had started ticked down second by second, preceding the automatic count down to weapon range. The count hit zero and Rhyta began her planned maneuver.

One of the triangle-sweep's strengths was that it effectively prevented escape for the merchant vessel. Any attempt to escape could be compensated for by the approaching ships. Even if a slightly greater delta-v were acquired, one of the three ships would always remain in weapon range.

Frost filled the *Melfar*'s cabin as the kinetic-drive applied a massive linear velocity change, diving directly at the ship marked Bravo. The weapon-engagement countdown instantly jumped to zero as the *Melfar* leapt towards the Bravo ship. Rhyta opened fire with the forward facing cannon. Each shot was an unstable Casimir Cell propelled forward by a miniature kinetic drive. While a direct collision was highly unlikely with even the most simple of evasive patterns, the nuclear-equivalent burst of raw energy could rip a ship in two if it came close enough. The burst charges were set according to timers – attempts at mass sensors were too inaccurate at the insane speeds that the cannon balls traveled.

At the same time, Melfar launched two missile swarms, one for Alpha and one for Charlie. Missiles were self-powered and traveled at saner speeds than the cannon shot. This allowed them time to maneuver and the ability to detect changes in the targeted ship's velocity vector. Like the cannon shot, the missiles would explode with a fury that would make any pyro-maniac proud, but, unlike the cannon shot, they were able to judge the best time to do the exploding.

Each swarm consisted of a dozen missiles. If the missiles were under automatic control, this would not be sufficient to overwhelm a Raven's point defense system. The equally auto-matic lasers mounted about the ship would be able to pick off the missiles before they closed to a dangerous proximity. However, if the missiles were under manual control, the situation was different. An intelligent mind, even burdened by the slight speed of light delay, could out-fox the point defense system and possibly bring one of the missiles into killing range.

Charlie clearly thought the missile swarm had a mind behind it. Or, perhaps as likely, did not trust in the efficacy of his point defense. Charlie's pursuit of *Melfar* was broken off as he swung out to give the missile swarm his full attention.

Alpha proved true to Rhyta's predictions and called the bluff of the missile swarm. The *Melfar* was diving into head-on-head combat with Bravo. As such, the pilot of the one-man ship could not divert any attention to control the missile swarms. He reasoned the swarms were meant to keep the three Ravens separate and thus negate the advantage in numbers they had. He thus flew straight for the dogfight that was erupting between Rhyta and Bravo, leaving his point defense to deal with the inbound missiles.

Unfortunately, Alpha did not know of Melfar's presence on the ship. The missile swarm heading for Charlie was on automatic, but the one heading to Alpha was under full manual control. Too late, the pilot of Alpha realized that a suspiciously large number of missiles were getting through his point defense network. Too late he tried to swing his Raven away from the three killing missiles that Melfar had managed to weave into blast range.

"Alpha down!" sang out Melfar as the hypothesized leader ship disintegrated in a ball of flames.

The viewscreens of the *Melfar* glowed white as a near blast temporarily overloaded their circuits. The Bravo Raven was proving a skilled fighter, having managed to squeeze a path through Rhyta's original firing pattern with only partial shield loss. His escape had driven him away from Charlie, however. Charlie had finished with his swarm of missiles to find himself out of range of both Melfar and Bravo, and to find Alpha a slowly expanding ball of vapour. Charlie accelerated towards the dogfight in the hopes of still coming to Bravo's rescue.

Bravo was having some trouble, however. The near blast which *Melfar* had sustained was not accidental. Rhyta had driven close to his firing pattern to avoid going in the direction which Bravo was trying to channel her. When the fires of Bravo's last salvo cleared, Rhyta was not where he expected her to be. He had fired a second salvo to close the gaps left intentionally in the first salvo, but those cannon shot exploded in vain. Instead, he found his own position assailed on all sides by glowing balls of death. He weaved for the only exit his on-board computer could track. As the glows of the nuclear hell-fire receded, allowing the blackness of space to show through, he found himself facing the *Melfar* direct on. And he realized that the exit he had found was not an accidental oversight mere milliseconds before Rhyta's timed shot dissolved his ship into component atoms.

Charlie entered weapon range of the plasma balls that marked the location of the dog fight. The plasma balls decayed to show no sign of Bravo. The *Melfar* was visible, however, just outside of weapon range. So were two swarms of missiles already streaking straight at him. This time, both swarms were under manual control.

* * *

The *Melfar* entered the the heliosphere of Asparg's Star at a stately pace. When traffic control requested their business, Rhyta calmly reported:

"This is Rhyta of the *Melfar* completing delivery of an antique painting on behalf of Pqz'ar of Asparg."

"We are afraid to report that Pqz'ar is under arrest for embezzlement of government funds. It seems he used public money to purchase rare art treasures from Earth to enhance his status. You'll have to deliver that painting to the authorities instead."

"By the Moon's silicon!" cursed Melfar, "I certainly hope this means we still get paid!"

# Chapter 23

*In which the Battleship* Wedzar *arrives at*
Menoetius. *An awkward reunion ensues*
*between Jorge and Fracks. Weistling makes no*
*progress with his next project.*

*W*eistling stared at the output on his data monitor and
cursed.

"You'd think I was trying to solve the Many-body Problem!
As if the very principles of mathematics are against me!" he
raged in response to a column of numbers that looked much like
they had in the previous test.

"After all these years of tinkering and observation, I finally
get a chance to build a tool. To use Menoetius as the artifact I
knew it to be. But does it work? No!" he continued with the
same bitterness that characterized his first outburst.

"I thought you were trying to solve the Many-body Problem.
Do the impossible. At least, that's what you told me when you
started this series of experiments," commented Kristina dryly.

"You had assured us that the formation of a macro-scale
wormhole was a violation of all of known physics when you
called us down for this demonstration," spoke Stewart.

"That was when I thought it would work," cursed Weistling.
"The array of instruments I had scanning every known frequency
during the event provided more than enough data. The method
involves a clever trick in the asymmetry of the super-
symmetries, exploiting the generation of the proper particles at
the event horizon to generate an imbalance, leading to massive

local concentration of virtual negative energy. The visible white lines were offset by another line in the deepest black. Depending on how much positive energy you pour into the positive half of the equation, you can form the wormhole faster or slower. That was a relatively energy-conscious opening we witnessed, for example. Given a good sized Casimir Cell, we should be able to open it in a tenth of the time."

"A matter of time again, perhaps?" replied Stewart, "Maybe that is your problem. Have you tried opening it slowly? May-hap some underlying physical restriction which you have not yet identified was the true source of the alien's lethargic entrance."

"Of course I tried opening it slowly. My first attempt was a mirror image of the hole we witnessed. The same parameters, but opening from normal space rather than hole-space..."

"Hole-space?" asked Jorge.

"Whatever we saw on the other side of that disc wasn't normal space. What do you want me to call it?"

"I think 'hyper-space' is customary," noted Stewart.

"Hyper-space implies extra-dimensionality," dismissed Weistling, "as far as I can tell, it's still three-space on the other side of the hole. Just a different three-space. Like it included three of those dimensions that the strings which make up our quarks are embedded in."

"How about over-space?" suggested Kristina.

"Both over and under imply a relative location. These spaces would be, as much as is meaningful, orthogonal to each other. It is like asking if up is left or right of forward."

"Well, according the the left-hand rule..." started Jorge, before he was cut off.

"Let's have a vote of all Phd-wielding Physicists in the room. Well, what do you know? Hole-space carries the vote with a unanimous backing! Hole-space it is."

"I think to be allowed to name it, you have to at least be able to reproduce it," Kristina said. "Otherwise, you will have shown no qualification any of us didn't already possess. Indeed, I believe Adom was the first to witness it, so perhaps he should have the deciding vote?"

"Could I name it after the Company?" asked Adom.

"NO!" shouted the rest of the room.

"By the tilt of Neptune, WORK!" yelled Weistling as the screen filled again with his latest tests. The numbers were all slightly different, but clearly not what he intended.

"I don't understand. I keep feeding more and more power into it, and no reaction."

"Is the black hole in the same state as when the original wormhole opened?" asked Kristina helpfully.

"Almost, but not quite." Weistling brought up a graph which meant little to those in the room. It showed a line of noise which, part way through the graph, grew in amplitude by about double. "About one day after the black hole closed, the virtual particle creation events almost doubled. They've remained at that level ever since. This would, theoretically, increase the power requirements to open a wormhole by a factor of eight. I've long since exceeded those power levels, however. Despite the fact that the applied field should dampen that line, it's been holding level despite my best efforts. There seems to be some form of feedback effect that is counteracting my attempts with a few milliseconds delay. But I can't figure out what is powering the feedback."

"A few milliseconds..." thought Stewart aloud, "you said with more power you could open the hole faster. What if you opened it within a millisecond?"

"Hmm..." Weistling performed a few quick calculations on his notebook. "Yes, some of the missiles still have Casimir Cells powerful enough..." Kristina shot a look at Adom, who, thankfully, had missed Weistling's inadvertent admission that the missiles had more than just their drive units cannibalized. "The problem is that you don't just need the power, but you need the field generators to project the power. Any of the ones we have on hand would blow out with magnitudes less power. I'd have to build one from scratch, which would take a long time. It'll probably be quicker if I figure out the source of this feedback and just eliminate that. After all, the aliens didn't have a problem."

Adom had not noticed Weistling's slip because he was responding to a chime from his wristwatch. "Weistling, do you mind if I put something on the monitor?"

"Sure."

Replacing the column of obstinate numbers was a text message.

```
To: Menoetius Station Manager
From: The Confederate Battleship Wedzar
Subject: Routine Patrol of Menoetius
Station

The Confederate Battleship Wedzar requests
permission to dock at Menoetius Station.
The Wedzar is engaged in a routine patrol
of the out-system, so will be available to
```

address any issues that have arisen with
the enforcement of Confederate Law.

While the Wedzar's supplies are military
issue, the Confederacy is always willing to
address any supply shortage that may be
present, provided doing so does not place
an undue strain on the Wedzar's flight
range.  Please reply with a list of any
needed supplies, services, and your
preferred parking orbit for the Wedzar.

Prosperity through Peace.
Captain Taler


Jorge paled when he read the missive.  Weistling reacted first, however.

"How fortunate!  Please put in a request for some machine-shop time!  If I can't build a powerful enough projector with the supplies of a battleship, I'll have to renounce my tinkers badge at once!"

"Think of others first for a change," snapped Kristina.  When Weistling looked confused, she explained.  "Recall the story Jorge gave of the scrape he just escaped?  It was a lieutenant of a certain battleship which double-crossed him and sent him here in hiding.  The battleship was the *Wedzar*."

"I'm sorry, Jorge.  We kept you here to run errand-boy for our mad-scientist, and now Fracks has caught up to you," sadly spoke Adom.

"Do not be sorry!  I'd have been sorry if I had chosen another port of call and missed the first alien contact that Humanity has made! Next to that, this is of no concern. In any case, my complaint is not with Captain Taler. The Confederacy still has no crime to pin on me." Jorge gave a jaunty smile which barely covered the unease underneath. His concern was genuine – if Fracks was close to the Captain, and the S'dar often ensured they would be, the Captain may take Fracks' side without looking too closely.

* * *

Captain Taler looked across the wood desk. Lieutenant Fracks was sitting at ease on a chair on the far side.

"I must hand it to you, lieutenant. You have actually become credit to the navy on this trip."

"I thank you, Captain," replied Fracks evenly. Lieutenant Fracks had thought long and hard on his trip back to the *Wedzar* from his humiliating debriefing on Earth. He discarded at once the possibility of trying to curry Captain Taler's favour by traditional forms of boot-licking. Not only would that not be in Fracks' established character, but Captain Taler had little interest in yes-men. Fracks realized that the only way he could insinuate himself into Captain Taler's good graces was by showing both hard work and competence. He started studying the navy training material again. Technically, naval personal were to be always studying the material, but he had let his studies flag. At first he was driven by the desire to curry favour and thus restore his good graces in the S'dar. To his shock, he discovered he actually enjoyed the work when well done. For one, his fellow officers quickly became a lot more amiable. And those under his command began to react out of loyalty rather than obedience.

"Menoetius Station isn't a small station, but there are less than a half dozen souls on it. I've thus decided to invite them for dinner this evening. We need an honour guard to bring them on board, and I have decided that you will be the head of it."

"I would be honoured, sir."

* * *

Weistling, Kristina, Stewart and Adom were gathered in the main dock of the station. They were all dressed in what constituted their finest attire. Adom wore a corporate business suit worth considerably more than his salary on Menoetius would justify. Weistling and Kristina both wore the flowing robes that were the official formal wear for academicians, despite their considerable impracticality in zero g. Thin memory-plastic wires in the robes continually applied a gentle force to straighten the robes down to the position they would have under gravity. The effect was disconcertingly as if the robes were alive. Stewart was wearing his crumpled tweed jacket.

The air lock light turned green. An almost silent hiss slid through the main dock. The Battleship clearly maintained regulation pressure. The main lock slowly opened.

Stepping out of the docking bay came four armed marines. Between them, attired in dress-whites, strode Lieutenant Fracks.

"Welcome to Menoetius!" greeted Adom.

"A pleasure to be here. A long trip, but the sight of that black hole is worth it."

"If more thought that way, there'd be more of us," sighed Adom. "This is Weistling, our physicist; Kristina, our xenologist; and Stewart, our philosopher."

"The RSVP said that there would be five of you?" prompted Fracks.

"That would be our other visitor – the pilot Jorge of the *Freia*," replied Adom, gesturing as Jorge stepped out of the shadows into view.

Fracks froze, his eyes fixed to those of Jorge. Jorge held Fracks' gaze with an unreadable stony expression. Fracks broke first and looked away, saying, "Now that we are all here, let us be off to the *Wedzar*. I understand it is a fine dinner that Captain Taler has prepared."

# Chapter 24

*In which the Redwing Strike Force invades.*

*C*ommander Uikar scanned his ready-screen nervously. The screen was filled with green entries – the forces under his command that had reported themselves prepared for the assault. Tension hung in the ship's bridge as the large chronometer slowly counted down the scant minutes remaining until they were to engage.

It had been a long wait. Certainly the longest time that Commander Uikar had to hold a position prior to an assault. His strike force was not used to having to wait for permission to clear a system of machine-infestation. The normal procedure had Uikar's Redwing sent to the doomed system with orders to engage at will.

The time holding in hole-space had been taxing on both Uikar and the people under his command. The shifting space that existed outside the ships often felt as if it also seeped in and contaminated the inside. Directions seemed to shift at random. All work had to be done with extra care because sudden waves of disorientation could cause up to seem as down without a moments warning. Uikar looked around at the officers on his bridge. Their normally bright plumage had faded with the weeks of anxious waiting for orders that seemed to never materialize.

Uikar fanned his crest in the universal signal of *Work Hard* and opened a wide-channel to the three sweeper-ships under his command.

"Fellow Praktonians!" he intoned. "I look at my ready-screen and see you have all reported ready to fight. But I look to your hearts and see the killing rage has dissipated! Have these weeks in directionless space caused your very souls to lose direction? Do your bones no longer remember the blood that was shed when we rid our home world of the would-be machine usurpers? And our shock when we learned that not all civilizations had been as successful as ours? Let other races talk of peace or pseudo-peace. We are here because we know there can be no peace. We are here to honour our warrior spirits and eradicate the machines wherever they can be found. Why do you mourn the week spent waiting for the Hegemony to make up its mind? That was the past. The now sees the wormhole opening and our driving the machine-quarry from this system into the abyss beyond!"

Uikar closed the channel. He scanned the bridge of his ship and was proud to see colour return to his officers' plumage. The Praktonians were a young race compared to the rest of the Galaxy. Strike patrols were usually comprised of young races – memories of their own recent battle with the machines had not yet faded in the face of the pseudo-peace. Still, Uikar did not like to invoke too deeply the raw emotion of that history. It could lead to blood lust, and in blood lust, mistakes were made. This was not the ceremonial battle prized by the Praktonians, but instead deadly war which required careful planning as much as valour. Fortunately, the careful planning could be left to those in the core systems, letting the Praktonians concentrate on the valour.

Uikar's under-officer, Vakar, asked the question which Uikar knew to be on everyone's mind.

"Sir, are we sure the enemy is still in the system?"

The thought of the enemy escaping while the Hegemony dawdled over the decision to attack had weighed heavily on the minds of all in the strike force. Fortunately, the question was now rhetorical. Which was no doubt why Vakar had voiced it – he was a good under-officer who understood well the finer points of morale.

"Do you not recall the lights dimming and the air circulation ceasing, Vakar? The Red Talon has been jamming the hole since our arrival. If the enemy fled, it would have been during the short window between the probe's appearance and our arrival. Their attempt to flee through the hole, thwarted by our jammer, shows that they did not avail themselves of that chance. The enemy is still there, Vakar. No doubt waiting scared with whatever base emotions their metal souls provide them, knowing that they are trapped, knowing that the cleansing flame of Praktonia will be coming for them."

In truth, it was Uikar who was worried. The jammer required only the square root of the power required to overload the jammer. The amount of power used by the enemy in an attempt to wrench open a wormhole had stressed their jammer to its design limits. Power had to be diverted from all other sources to keep the hole jammed in face of the desperate onslaught. Desperate could be the only word for it – the enemy had likely exhausted its stored power reserves with the last attempt. No further attempts to open the wormhole had been detected, leading Uikar's techs to conclude that the enemy's power was finally exhausted.

Still, Uikar was tempted to summon reinforcements, despite the fact that further delay to battle might ruin his crew. The power used suggested that it was not just a simple space station that they faced. The probe's scan of the system had been thorough. It had revealed a dense constellation of observation satellites, all linked via tight beams to the station, in close orbit about the hole. The amount, and redundancy, of the sensors showed an almost paranoid interest in the doings of the black hole. Another, smaller, cluster of sensors was spotted slowly sweeping through the heliosphere on what seemed to be, of all things, a search pattern. The purpose was unknown, but that wasn't Uikar's concern. The distance of those sensors meant they could be ignored until the main battle was over – their light cones would prohibit their involvement for tens of hours. They were frustrating, however. A clean sweep of a system required the systematic destruction of all artifacts. Flying out to the heliosphere and back would likely waste as much time as they had already spent hiding in hole-space.

Uikar's compromise to his concerns was to choose a more conservative plan for the attack. Normally, the strike force would shut the wormhole behind them to prevent any easy escape for their prey. In this battle, however, Uikar would keep the wormhole open so that telemetry data could be sent back to the core worlds. This mission had enough unusual features that, if they were overwhelmed by the defenders, the High Council would likely want as much additional data as possible. Not that he planned on failing.

The large chronometer showed slightly more than three minutes remained.

"Deactivate the jammer on my mark!" barked Uikar. "Mark!"

Uikar's status screen showed the power demands of the jammer abate in milliseconds. The power was re-diverted to charging the capacitors for the wormhole generator. The moment of no-return had passed. The cessation of the jamming signal could be detected from the other side of the black hole. The strike force was ready for any signs of the enemy attempting to build an escape wormhole. The Red Beak had the task of using its jammer if that occurred, letting the Red Talon's wormhole generator fully charge. Uikar could have had the Red Beak open a wormhole rather than waiting for the Red Talon, but he wanted to have his other ships' capacitors full at the start of the battle. Due to the speed of light delays to the station, even the few minutes warning provided by the jammer ceasing would not grant sufficient time to ready a coherent counter attack. Still, Uikar regretted having to give any warning at all.

The chronometer reached zero.

"Open the wormhole!" commanded Uikar. The Red Talon's capacitors drained as the wormhole generator was activated. Uikar had ordered the fastest possible opening speed, even though that would leave the Red Talon with drained energy reserves. He intended to minimize the warning the enemy already had. Even using all the immense power storage of the Red Talon's capacitor arrays, the wormhole would take a minimum of thirty seconds to open. Uikar took advantage of the delay to instruct his other ships with the commands that they already knew by heart.

"Red Beak, sweep in first. I want the observational satellites turned to dust before they know the wormhole has opened! Red Feather, you are second. Verify location of the station and launch a full salvo – set the missile salvo to en-globe all conceivable delta-vees."

"Red Talon will bring up the rear and perform a full system scan for any new surprises. If the information from the High Council is right, I don't want the Red Talon to even warm up its missile bays."

The swirling black lines, spinning ever faster, consolidated into a solid black disc, revealing behind the light of the star of their target system. Red Beak leapt forward – its atomic drive flaring brightly as it entered normal space. Seconds later, Red Feather took its turn to fly into the system. Hundreds of bright stars flew from the launch bays of the Red Beak as it launched its micro-missiles. The observational satellites were in the predicted locations so reprogramming of the micro-missiles was not necessary. As the Red Feather passed through the black disk, the system lit up with hundreds of low yield nuclear explosions. Incoming telemetry showed Uikar that the micro-missiles were finding their marks.

The Red Talon's drives sang as they powered up, pushing the Red Talon at last into normal space and into what was quickly becoming a maelstrom of electromagnetic noise. The Red Feather reported locating the target space station and a dozen brighter stars launched from its launch bays. These were full size missiles. Each one with the best guidance system that the Praktorian's could devise short of AI. Each missile had its own atomic engine that accelerated it at crushing speeds to its target. The atomic engine was also the warhead, set to destroy itself in a nuclear inferno when the pre-programmed conditions were met. The Red Feather had set the missiles to saturate the space around the station. A station was unlikely to be equipped with a drive, and thus unlikely to be able to dodge, but Uikar did not become a commander by taking unnecessary chances.

A sudden twist let Uikar know that the Red Talon had entered normal space. The sense of unease that had faded into the subconscious was lifted, bringing a sigh of relief to the beaks of his crew. The telemetry data from the other ships continued to pour in, now coupled with the Red Talon's superior sensor readouts. Uikar verified that an outgoing signal was still being sent back through the wormhole. If nothing else, the High Council could be entertained with some fine fireworks, as the current situation looked like overkill.

Uikar's eyes stopped instantly when they ran across the unexpected datum. The station, the constellation of satellites around the black hole, and the cluster of satellites scanning the heliosphere – they were all accounted for and in the right location. That ship, however, was not. The ship was in a slightly unstable parking orbit around the black hole, trailing the station by a few degrees of arc. Uikar guessed that the source of the attempt escape attempt had been discovered. No doubt this ship entered in the post-probe window and was trapped behind their jamming wall. It was a big ship. Twice the size of Uikar's own flag ship, its diameter was half the size of the space station. No doubt that accounted for the powerful capacitors that almost opened a wormhole despite Uikar's blockade.

"Red Talon, we are to engage the new ship directly. Red Feather, chase your missiles to the station and verify destruction, then join us against the new ship. Red Beak, take a flanking route and engage the new ship stat," ordered Uikar.

The Red Talon responded to Uikar's orders as if he had the flight-stick in his wings, rather than the wings of a subordinate. The scream of the atomic drive reverberated through the ship as it accelerated in a tight arc to the novel threat.

"Launch missiles with standard en-globing." With the light-second delay, the ship might already be accelerating in response to their arrival. Fortunately, more mass meant more inertia. Even better, the power scanners showed the new ship's drive was still shutdown. Starting an atomic drive from a cold would cost the ship a few minutes, by which time it would be reduced to ash. Uikar wondered at the foolishness of the Captain which hadn't reacted to the cessation of the jamming signal by powering up the drive. He didn't wonder long. One took the luck that one could find.

A dozen stars sped away from the Red Talon at speeds that would crush any organic being instantly. The missiles had been launched. A matching dozen stars left the Red Beak, arcing in from a different angle, the two clusters cutting off any hope of escape.

A chime announced an incoming communication from the Red Feather: "Missiles approaching the station. ETA is one minute."

Uikar glanced at his tactical plot and saw that the tight grouping of the Red Feather's missiles had spread out into a spherical pattern. The leading missiles were accelerating slightly faster to allow the entire missile globe to explode at once.

The new ship still hadn't responded to the attack.

Suddenly, the Red Feather's missiles disappeared from the tactical screen when still thirty seconds from their target. A ball of plasma had exploded in the middle of their formation, obliterating the entire lot.

The Red Beak's missiles and the Red Talon's missiles suffered similar fates seconds later.

"Mines!" shouted Uikar. "Full reverse!" Uikar's mind raced. *How could they have predicted our missiles' flight plans well enough to have mined the approach path?*

The Red Feather disappeared in a ball of plasma. The Red Beak was half way through its braking turn when it also disappeared in a ball of plasma. A final ball of plasma blossomed in the location of the Red Talon cutting short the telemetry signal. No force holding it open any longer, the wormhole in Menoetius collapsed.

# Chapter 25

*In which a pleasant dinner party on board the*
Wedzar *is interrupted by rude guests.*

*T*he conversation at the Captain's dinner had finished covering the latest machinations of the powers on Earth when Captain Taler inquired after the happenings on the station.

"I could not help but notice that Weistling looks ready to burst," remarked Captain Taler affably. "Could it be that your station has some news for us? Rare is the gossip that can travel inwards against the pressure of Earth society, but that just makes it all the more remarkable."

"It is more than just gossip," commented Kristina, toying with her wine glass. She was glad to see that Weistling had held his tongue this long. She had promised dire retribution if he usurped her right to announce the discovery her experiment had precipitated. "What we have to report is the sort of news that will be announced over the high priority channels on your return to Earth. We have solved the riddle of Menoetius."

"Indeed? After all these decades the solution is found? You then found the natural process that could generate a black hole of Menoetius' light mass?" queried Taler.

"I am sorry, Captain, but it was no natural process. Menoetius is most definitely an alien artifact," Kristina stated forcefully.

"That is surprising! I am not an expert by study, but I have traveled most of known space in my decades in the Navy. And in those decades we have found no alien life form that showed even the slightest glimmer of intelligence. We have found no artifacts of lost civilizations that had crumbled to ruins. We have detected no signals of alien races seeking to speak with us, or with anyone. I have come to the conclusion that Humanity's rise to intelligence is unique. The nature of intelligence seems to be counter-evolutionary – the ability to question one's role in the universe leads to energy wasted on soul searching that could be more efficiently spent on survival. Indeed, we need only look at our own history, at the number of times our own intellect was almost our undoing, to wonder why our simian ancestors ever bothered to breed more clever descendants."

"A relatively common view, even among xenologists, I fear," admitted Kristina. "Unfortunately, you need to update your universe view with the same alacrity that ancient physicists had to update theirs in reaction to the kinetic drive. As I said, it is an alien artifact."

"And, if I may be so bold as to ask, what evidence do you have that supports that? Is it possible to explain it to laymen like ourselves?" Captain Taler gestured to include the others at the Captain's table, fellow officers who were following the conversation with alert ears.

"The evidence is accessible to anyone. With your permission, we can show it on that screen?" asked Kristina. Captain Taler nodded. Kristina made a few quick notes in her notebook and the screen cleared to show a floating image of Menoetius.

A pin point of white light showed up in the center of the black hole. It spread out into a line and started swirling. Soon, it coalesced into a disc from which an alien ship sped out under its atomic plume. Kristina sped up the playback to cover its sweep and hurried departure.

"This is a joke, isn't it?" replied one of the lieutenants at the table. "Some computer generated recording you put together in your spare time to trick would be visitors?"

"I can see why you would think that," replied Adom evenly, preempting what looked like a less civil response from Kristina or Weistling. "A bunch of scientists locked away on a dead-end space station monitoring an unresponsive black hole would seem prime candidates for space-craziness. I am not a scientist, however, but a manager. Whatever my faults, they do not extend to imagining fanciful tales of alien races. Further, Jorge was also present as a witness to these events. While solo traders like Jorge are even more likely to start imagining ghosts between the stars, I do not think he was on this station long enough to be corrupted wholly by us."

"As I am sure you know, incredible claims require incredible proof," stated Captain Taler. "While I am willing to trust your integrity and believe that this happened, I hope you understand that I will have to do the opposite of broadcasting this with high priority on my return? Instead, I will have to keep it secret until we can get a third party here to verify your recordings' integrity and physical plausibility.

"Let us leave aside questions of verification. I request all at this table take what our guests say as true and question accord-ingly. I have a question: that anachronistically atomic powered ship changed its course at a very high cost. Do you have any idea why it did so?"

"We sent the standard First Contact signals when we received its wide band transmission. It had barely received the start of the First Contact procedure when it aborted its scan and made the fastest possible return to the wormhole."

"Quite odd. It must have detected the presence of the space station, or the presence of the observational satellites, before then. Those did not spook it, but the First Contact signal did. That would suggest it knew what the signal was." Then, in an apparent non-sequitur, Taler added, "The First Contact procedures are quite ancient – they predate the Confederacy, you know?"

"Beyond the disk seemed to be some glowing plasma – what was that?" asked a flight officer.

"That was the first peek that Humanity has had into the twisted dimensions that lie beside our own. A peek into... hole-space!" announced Weistling, who felt that he had waited long enough to provide his own views.

"Hole-space?" asked Captain Taler, incredulous, "surely you mean hyper-space? Or over-space? Or under-space? I thought the nature of mysterious spaces on the other side of wormholes were well defined in science fiction?"

"Those other terms are all very misleading about the actual nature of the space on the other side of the wormhole. It might not even be properly called a wormhole, as it doesn't bridge two points in real space. Instead, it turns a corner into one of the tightly wrapped dimensions orthogonal to our own, the small nature of which no doubt allows instant travel to other similarly created wormholes. The speed of light is plenty fast enough when one's entire universe is infinitely smaller than an atom."

"Hole-space, it is then," conceded Taler. "Have you determined how this disk was created? Is it possible for us to open a wormhole ourselves?"

"Yes." spoke Weistling with confidence. "I acquired more than enough data to know how to replicate the effect. The theoretical framework seems solid enough to allow us to generate our own wormholes. The practical execution has been lacking, however. Since the alien craft left the system, some of the low-order noise that the wormhole opening depends on has changed in character. I thought I could overcome it with sufficient energy, but some form of feedback effect canceled out my attempts. I've designed plans for a wormhole generator powerful enough to operate within the window before the feedback effect occurs, but I need specialized equipment to do so."

"Ah, so that is the reason for the unusual request for machine-shop time? Very well. Our schedule would permit us to stay in system long enough to see if your plans are successful. With that proof, we could announce directly your discovery without having to attempt to shroud it in a mantle of secrecy. Information tends to leak through those mantles, in my experience. I do have another question however. One for Kristina. You all keep referring to the spacecraft as alien. It is alien in the sense that it is not Confederate. But why are you convinced it is not human?"

Kristina thought for a moment before replying. "First, you will note it possesses the secret of wormhole generation. That implies that it is familiar with black holes. The only black hole in human-known space is here, and we have extensive logs of every second we've been in orbit here. If anyone had developed that generator here, the Confederacy would already know about it. Second, you'll note the use of atomics as a propulsion device. If it were human, it would surely use kinetics instead. Finally, and most convincingly..."

Kristina was cut off by a loud series of beeps from Weistling's wristwatch. Weistling had opened his note book and was eagerly looking at what it showed him.

"That had better be important, Weistling!" spoke Kristina coolly.

"The interference in the black hole! It has stopped! The noise is back to pre-event levels. I should be able to open the black hole with my current equipment now!"

"That will have to wait, Weistling," said Adom evenly, "We are at dinner now. There will be time for your experiments when we get back to the station."

"But the noise might return!" whined Weistling. He did put away the notebook though, and the discussion ceased as dessert was brought in. The dessert was slices of cheesecake with chocolate flakes on top and drizzled with a raspberry sauce.

"I have not had cheesecake in.... I don't know how many years," breathed Adom as the slice of cake was placed before him. "I am most amazed that you can provide such delicacies on a working ship."

"Good food masses as much as poor food," commented Captain Taler. "The Confederacy's job is to enforce civilization. As such, it is imperative that we remember what civilization is."

The first mouthfuls were half way to their mouths when klaxons rang through the ship.

"ALERT! ALERT! ALL HANDS ON DECK!"

Captain Taler jumped to his feet and shot through a side door before any of the guests could react. They turned to each other with questioning gazes. Weistling slowly turned his notebook around so that everyone could see it. On screen was the image of Menoetius slowly revolving. In the center was a bright white line.

* * *

Captain Taler shot onto the bridge at a high speed. His hand reached out to grab the edge of his command chair and he used his momentum to swing himself into his seat.

"Report!" he barked.

The officer-on-watch, Merdith, gave a quick account. This consisted first of gesturing to the main screen where the *Wedzar*'s view of Menoetius was writ large. In the center of the hole was a fast spinning brilliant white swirl.

"A bright light was seen in the center of the black hole. When it grew into a solid white line, I called the alert. It has since spun into this," reported Merdith with quick words.

"Send me to the dead-zones of Earth! They were telling the truth. Prepare yourselves – we are about to have visitors!" warned Taler.

As if his words were a cue, the disk coalesced into solidity. Through the white shimmering veil they could see the chaos of so-called hole space. A strangely shaped ship slid out of the disk and into real space. A brilliant plume of atomic exhaust followed it; the ship accelerating hard with the full might of its engines.

"Ready battle stations!" commanded Captain Taler redundantly. "Acquire lock but hold fire pending my orders."

"Sir, at this range we will not be able to predict their position closely enough to fire?" questioned the weapons officer.

"Assume a ballistic course. We have reason to believe they are running only on atomics, so have limited maneuverability. Communications: any signal from our visitors yet?"

"No sir," replied Hark, the communications officer, "Alpha ship is under radio silence."

"Alpha ship has launched missiles!" alerted Tactical. "A salvo of approximately one hundred independently propelled devices. All using atomics, sir!"

"We do not yet know they are missiles," cautioned Captain Taler, "it is imperative that we do not accidentally invoke hostilities."

The view of Menoetius turned white as simultaneous nuclear explosions atomized Weistling's carefully built array of observational satellites. The researchers, Adom, and Jorge, still in the dining room, cursed when their view went black. When Weistling reset the view to show the feed from the station's observational equipment, he shouted in fury. The strength of his bellow could be heard even in the bridge, where Captain Taler remarked dryly, "I believe we may now categorize those as missiles."

"Sir! Second hostile has entered the system!" Tactical reported as a new ship slipped through the white disk. It, too, was under heavy acceleration and trailed a plume of atomic dust. The tactical computer assigned it Bravo.

"Bravo ship has deployed... shuttles?" reported Tactical as a dozen new atomic plumes separated from Bravo and accelerated into space.

"Not at those accelerations. Anyone inside would be paste against a wall," noted Captain Taler. "I'd categorize them as larger missiles. What is their target?"

"The missiles appear to be set for an en-globing pattern of the station. If their yield scales with their size, any one of them would take out the station. They appear to be set to assume a ballistic course for the station. The fire pattern encompasses course deviations caused by up to five gees of acceleration."

"A logical safety margin for anyone who thinks in terms of atomic drives. Weapons, I want a one-shot one-kill solution for those missiles."

"Roger," reported Weapons. This time there was no questioning the long range. The behaviour of the ships had convinced the weapons officer that a simple ballistic prediction would suffice. Captain Taler hoped this was not just an elaborate ruse.

"Third ship has entered system, Sir!" alerted Tactics. The ship, labeled Charlie, slid through the wormhole.

"Charlie ship has launched! Alpha ship has launched!" Two dozen new atomic plumes, in two groups, slid out from the pair of ships. The Bravo ship continued to follow its own set of missiles inbound to the station.

"Tactics. Run a calculation. If we were an atomic drive ship, how many gees would we need to escape the oncoming barrage?"

The tactics officer, to her credit, did not take more than a moment to reply. Clearly she had already run the calculations for evasion under kinetic drive, and hence could easily solve for the velocity change required. "197 gees to escape by the most optimum route, sir. That would assume they don't have another salvo planned to plug that escape. To get sufficient options to render our motion unblockable to further salvos would require 273 gees."

"Ah, thank you. I think this has gone on long enough," said Captain Taler evenly. "Our visitors are clearly hostile, and speed of light means any diplomacy would have to wait until the station was destroyed or they had closed unacceptably. Weapons! Destroy in turn the incoming missile clouds on my mark. Then destroy Bravo ship, its path to the space station is troubling. I want Alpha and Charlie to see this before you set something close enough to them to disable them. Hopefully they will then be interested in responding to the First Contact Protocols."

"Yes, Sir. On your mark."

"Mark," said Taler coolly.

The weapons officer had decided on firing the main cannon rather than using more expensive missiles. While the enemy targets had some maneuverability, the light-delay and their potential acceleration was low enough that it was easy to plot a solution that could encompass both them and their entire potential divergence from a ballistic course. *Wedzar*'s main cannon coughed as it spat out a hyper-velocity Casimir Cell timed to detonate in the midst of the station bound missiles. It fired again, and again, as each target was selected, solved for, and shot at. While the *Wedzar* had enough hands and cannon to eliminate all the threats with a single broadside, Captain Taler's request for a timed destruction meant only one cannon was necessary. The Weapons Officer reserved this task for himself so he could be sure the correct speed of light delays were accounted for.

To see the success of their shots, they had to wait for light from the explosions to make its way back to them. Normal weapon range was predicated on this light delay being low enough that the enemy's interim motion would not result in a guaranteed miss. Captain Taler was hoping that the limited maneuverability of atomic drives had extended this range considerably. In any case, if the opponents did have kinetic drives, he intended to flush them out sooner than later.

The first shot destroyed the station bound missiles. The two flights heading at the *Wedzar* then vanished in their own clouds of hellish plasma. A direct hit on Bravo ship overloaded whatever shields it might have and left only traces of dust behind. The *Wedzar*'s cannon was silent now – the remaining shots already fired. Alpha ship, and then Charlie ship, gained their own balls of plasma. The weapons officer had been careful with his plotting. The plasma balls were sufficiently far from each ship that, while the shields might have failed, the ships should remain mostly intact. With proper emergency precautions and some luck there could even be survivors.

When the clouds of plasma around Alpha and Charlie dissipated they did not reveal broken, limping, ships, however. They revealed nothing. The ships had been reduced to their component atoms as surely as if the shots had been direct hits.

"I thought I said I wanted survivors?" remarked Captain Taler.

"I'm sorry, sir," apologized the weapons officer. "I plotted my solution assuming they had reasonable shields. Their shields must not have been up."

Captain Taler realized too late that what he meant as a joke could cause offense. "Or, they didn't have shields. Your firing patterns were perfect. We have at least learned more about the capability of our foe."

"Sir, the wormhole seems to be collapsing!" reported Tactical.

"That it does," remarked Captain Taler as the wormhole slowly spun down. "Communication, please bring our guests to the bridge. I think they will want to discuss what we have just witnessed."

When the communication officer had brought Jorge, Weistling, Kristina, Stewart, and Adom to the bridge, Captain

Taler turned to face them, a playback of the battle playing in a loop on the main screen.

"I think questions of the veracity of your claims are mostly settled. That altercation well exceeded what you could perform as a hoax. Indeed, even if the attack was a hoax, it implies that you successfully created wormholes, which is more than enough of a discovery."

"I would never destroy my sensors for a hoax," was Weistling's response. "I wish you hadn't taken so long to destroy those invaders – my sensors might still be functioning!"

"I was not about to attack someone who had not shown any hostile behaviour," barked Captain Taler. "Not to mention that your sensors were already destroyed by the time we saw the first ship enter the system. In any case, I suspect you will see those sensors repaid a thousand fold. This black hole is now of highest priority to the Confederacy."

"I find it sad that our second contact with aliens results in a battle," commented Stewart.

"They were the one's that shot first – at my sensors!" retorted Weistling.

"Perhaps this is their system? And they were just performing house cleaning?" suggested Stewart.

Captain Taler cut off the growing argument. "First, it is not at all apparent that these are aliens. Occam's razor suggests we consider other possibilities first. For example, a lost colony of Earth that had regressed and lost the secret to the kinetic drive, but gained the secret of wormhole travel. Second, the enemy knows how to get to us. The question is: do we know how to get to them?"

"As I said before, the technology to open a wormhole is well within our reach," replied Weistling. "The only reason I had not already opened one was that noise, which has dissipated. It is then just a matter of learning how to navigate hole-space to discover where they are in the universe."

"Good. The next order of priority is to alert Earth. The *Wedzar* will have to picket here in case a second attack is made."

"Too bad we cannot avoid that," commented Adom, "the more blood that spills, the less chance of peaceful reconciliation."

"Why don't we just lock the black hole?" suggested Weistling innocently.

"Lock?" queried Captain Taler.

"Yes. What they did to us. I just figured it out. It explains the supposed feedback. It wasn't feedback from a natural process, but rather from a noise generator on their ship on the other side of the wormhole. With the resources of the *Wedzar*, we could easily construct a noise generator that would prevent wormholes from being opened. The power to suppress the noise is the square of the power applied by the noise generator, so with the station's main Casimir Cell, we could keep the wormhole locked against almost all conceivable energy outputs."

"Excellent news. I want you to build both a wormhole lock and a wormhole generator, in that order. After we verify with the generator that the lock is functional, the *Wedzar* can proceed to the source of this disturbance."

"You mean to enter the wormhole and track them back?" asked Kristina.

"No. As it happens, I have a very good idea where they are in real space," replied Captain Taler, absently tapping a sealed envelope by his command chair.

* * *

"If that doesn't inspire your art, I don't know what would," spoke Rhyta softly as the last plasma ball faded to black. They had watched the battle, a few hours later than real time, from their position in a slow orbit well off the elliptic. All non-passive systems had been powered down prior to the *Wedzar*'s entry into the system.

"What? What happened?" was Melfar's delayed response as he shifted his focus from the video game he had been playing.

# Chapter 26

*In which the High Council of the Hegemony of the Organics meets to choose its course of action. A dangerous gambit is determined to be the only viable route.*

The High Council usually only met in person during official ceremonies, such as the admission of a new member to the council. When Regars, the current leader of the council, called for a meeting and demanded the physical presence of all members, it marked the first time in ten thousand years that a physical meeting had been called outside of routine formalities.

Meetings over electronic telepresence required little warning: members of the High Council were always ready to clear their agendas for urgent matters requiring their decisions. Physical meetings, however, required considerable logistic planning. Attendance at a physical meeting implied a much larger break in the participant's busy schedule. Travel to the meeting often required days, as many members tolerated a few minutes light-lag in telepresence meetings in order to live on their home worlds rather than in black-hole orbiting stations. A physical meeting required them to travel to the black-hole itself at speeds that their flesh could withstand. This turned minutes of light lag into days or weeks of travel time, depending on the robustness of their physiology.

The logistics of the meeting itself were simpler. The Core Station had a room always prepped for just this purpose. Each of the High Council's myriad digestive and respiratory systems were taken into account, and plenty of supplies for each member's needs were stored. Separate rooms were available for each member to relax in their native atmospheric pressure and mix of chemicals.

The meeting room itself was kept pressurized to a value that, inevitably, was uncomfortable to all present. The atmosphere of the meeting room was a mix of noble gases. Each participant had to bring a respirator to add their own balance of reactive gases to the mix.

Regars began the meeting with the appropriate ceremony.

"Are all of the High Council gathered in this one place?" he asked. The words were shown in the common tongue of the Hegemony on each High Council's notebook. Respirators inhibited speech; all communication was done via text.

Regars' notebook display checked off each of the members of the High Council as they registered their presence.

"This meeting is sealed," announced Regars. Shock appeared on some of the councilor's faces. Regars noted which members showed shock – it showed an astonishing lack of foresight to have failed to realize that such an unusual thing as a physical meeting could only be called for one reason: privacy. Physical meetings were common during the period of total-war with the Hegemony of Machines. A face-to-face meeting in a suitably sealed area was the only proven way to ensure security. Telepresence meetings, with the content being sent across space, through scores of wormholes and hundreds of routers, provided too many opportunities to eavesdrop.

"All communication in and out of this room has been cut off. Our powerlines are now isolated from the station's grid. Please set your notebooks to delete-on-display." Regars waited until each member's notebook had reported itself as being in delete-on-display mode.

Without further preamble, Regars began the meeting. "We are not gathered here today for ceremony. We are gathered here today to carry out the task that the Hegemony has entrusted to us. The successful prosecution of the War with the Machines."

"I thought our task was the maintenance of the pseudo-peace?" asked K'jar. K'jar had been one of those shocked when the meeting was sealed. A short creature, half a meter at his highest, and covered with coarse thick blue hair, K'jar looked like a blue moss-covered rock when sitting stationary. No mobility appendages were visible in the rest state, all five of them being tucked against the body, and their hair serving to blend them in with the body. This allowed K'jar's ancestors to not reveal the direction they faced to prey or predators, and thus be able to leap in an unexpected direction. In modern, civilized, time periods, it had the effect of making it notoriously difficulty to read the emotions of K'jar's race. K'jar, however, had rocked back and forth as he asked the question. Resgar knew K'jar well enough to recognize that as a sign of uneasiness. K'jar clearly realized that his statement was incorrect, and that he likely should have known better. Resgar was glad he voiced it rather than staying silent – no doubt others had the same thought.

"For hundreds of thousands of years, that is what we have done. That was not the task the High Council was assigned during the formation of the Hegemony. The original task, and, as it has never been changed, still the task, of the High Council is to successfully prosecute the War with the Machines. Hundreds of thousands of years ago, our ancestors determined that the best way to accomplish that task was through the pseudo-peace. We have thus sought to maintain the pseudo-peace in the ensuing time.

"It is not lightly that I draw attention to the precise distinction between our stated purpose and what we have done. In normal circumstances, it is enough to seek the maintenance. In extreme times, however, it is important that we return to our original mission and re-examine the reasons that led us to the pseudo-peace. If those reasons no longer hold, we should not maintain the pseudo-peace.

"The extreme situation I refer to is the the tactical feed we received from a recent strike force."

The main screen of the meeting room, along with each participant's notebooks, cleared to reveal the messages sent by the ill-fated Red Wing Strike Force. The High Council watched as the strike force moved into the system. They saw the tactical summary at the bottom of the screen that explained how the attack pattern consisted of considerable overkill. The expected probability of failure generated by the Core's tactical experts in response to the known data was as near zero as possible in a universe containing uncertainty. One of the most likely failure conditions was the unexpected supernova of the star wiping out both forces. Thus, when the elements of the strike force winked out one by one in glowing puffs of plasma, there were a series of gasps from the High Council. The display ended abruptly with only the text: "SIGNAL LOST" on the screen.

"The destruction of a strike force is rare, but not unheard of. The tactical summary mis-predicting the success of the strike force, even with the advantage of hind sight, is much more worrying. This has never occurred during the pseudo-peace when the strike force's opponents were just rogue AI or rogue Organic organizations. The only times it occurred was during the total-war. Even then, it was rare, and each time it marked the development of a fundamental shift in methodology by the Machines."

"This system was already an anomaly, correct?" inquired the pink-skinned Henkbar.

"Yes. That was partly the reason we have the tactical data. The commander of the Red Wing strike force was uneasy when he was forced to maintain position while we determined what to do with this system. A routine probe found the system occupied with an unregistered space station. The challenge code was not met with a response, but instead the station feigned ignorance and replied with what appeared to be a First Contact protocol. That it could be a genuinely new civilization seemed unbelievable. Still, we took every precaution. Expert opinions all concurred that no intelligent life could have formed in that system, and that the only way a new civilization could have got to the system would have been through the black hole. Inquiries were made with our counterparts in the Machine Hegemony and they denied all knowledge of the system, recommending its destruction for the same reasons we had. The High Council thus resolved to declare the unknown space station an outlaw element of one of the two Hegemonies, and hence sentenced it to destruction."

"Why then this meeting? So the rogue element proved a bit more intractable than usual. Determine their technique – the use of mines does seem a likely possibility – and attack again with greater force," spat Xzarop, a large purple slug who had little like for the lack of humidity in the meeting room.

"Mines would explain the witnessed events," conceded Resgar. "Precisely placed mines with proximity detectors could achieve the effect seen. The mines would have to both be heavily cloaked and have an explosive power a few orders of magnitude higher than our standard mines. However, the routes flown by the Red Wing strike force were appropriately randomized. There is no way the defender could have known a priori which route they would use to attack. To cover a sufficient envelope, the minefield would have to be light seconds in diameter and contain millions of mines. With those levels of resources, the defenders could have equipped a fleet of ships and easily won the battle in a more traditional way. In any case, such a large resource expenditure suggests strongly this is an act of the Machine Hegemony, not just some rogue element.

"Second, as for the counter attack. We would have done so. Except the wormhole is jammed."

"But that means they are still there? Why did they not take advantage of the chance to escape?" asked K'jar.

"A good question. Our strategists expected us to find a system scoured clean of any trace of the Machine's doings. Their continued presence can only mean that this system is somehow critical to whatever the Machine's are now planning," answered Resgar.

"And the Machine Hegemony continues to deny all knowledge of this system?" asked K'jar, rocking back and forth.

"I'm afraid it has escalated beyond that," confessed Resgar. "Our continued inquiries on the matter have led them to claim that we are trying to manufacture an incident. The pseudo-peace is already strained by this event.

"If they were unable to evacuate that system, it implies that they have assets that are not evacuable. The ship detected could easily ferry out components of that space station if necessary. The most likely reason to not escape would be that the speed of light precluded a timely evacuation: they have interests in nearby star systems as well," commented Fdar. Resgar noted that Fdar seemed unperturbed with the developments. The three-legged, three-eyed race that Fdar belonged to had entered the Hegemony prior to the pseudo-peace so could provide the race-memory of what total-war meant.

"That matches the reasoning of our strategists," replied Resgar. "They conclude, with a high probability, that this must be the black hole outpost to a star system not on the wormhole network. The existence of the mysterious survey satellites as far out as the heliosphere speak strongly of some sort of extra-system interest. An interstellar trip without a wormhole could easily mean a ten year lag if the evacuation was called for. Not being able to abandon the outpost, they have to hold it until reinforcements come."

"Reinforcements? I thought the Machine Hegemony denied involvement. An attack on picket of the hole-space side of the system would be a clear statement of involvement," stated K'jar.

"You are assuming they are denying involvement with the intent to cover up their involvement in this system. If that was the case, they would have been better served by clearing the system and abandoning their interstellar assets. I believe they are denying involvement to buy time. When this mystery project comes to fruition, they will move openly and restart total-war."

The members of the High Council from younger civilizations, to whom the pseudo-peace was the status quo and total-war ancient history, paled in their myriad of ways.

"If we are not to lose this new round of total-war," continued Resgar, "it is imperative that we shut down this project before it is completed. And that we do so before the Machine Hegemony feels itself strong enough to openly claim involvement."

"The plan seems still clear," spittled Xzarop, "we ignore the horrendous energy costs and charge up a Wormhole Saw. We assemble a massive fleet of ships, cut open a wormhole before their jammer can respond, and then flood the system with missiles. One atomic holocaust later, the system is clean and problem solved."

"Except...," replied Resgar slowly, "there will still be that outpost circling another star. If that outpost were the actual field of operations, they could continue their research unabated. Without a rogue presence in the system to justify our own presence, we would have to leave the system quickly. The Machine Hegemony's recent transmissions make it clear that they expect us to leave swiftly when the problem is dealt with – as I mentioned, they are contending that we are inventing this problem to justify our actions in this system. In twenty or thirty years, the outpost could safely return to the system and take their results back to the Machines via the wormhole. Or, more likely, if they are ready to move openly, they could just create a black hole in the system that they are in, and transit back that way."

"Unless we create the black hole first," replied Fdar. "We could, from hole-space, create a black hole in the system of the suspected outpost. Those heliosphere satellites were completing a sensor sweep, suggesting they began the sweep on the other side of the heliosphere. Such a sweep could have been done to ensure there were no deep-space surprises lurking in the system. It would be sensible to start from the direction of most importance: the direction of the interstellar outpost. As it happens, a half dozen light years along that direction is a system with a habitable world that we could target with our black hole generators."

"A habitable world that might have intelligent life!" shouted Henkbar, "Black hole generation is only done from real-space for a very good reason: to do otherwise might condemn a nascent civilization to destruction!"

"Not to mention, any opening of new black holes in this space will be read as an expansionistic policy by the Machines. The Machine Hegemony will have no choice but to conduct a reprisal. And they will be sure to target a world that is of importance to us," replied Resgar.

"As you said earlier," spoke Fdar calmly, "the Machines clearly believe that this outpost could tip total-war in their favour, despite the numerous proofs to the opposite. Otherwise they would not have risked so much already. We must be willing to accept the loss of a world or two if it can preempt the Machines developing this technology."

"You would condemn billions," said Henkbar quietly.

"To prevent the loss of a total-war that would see all Organic life destroyed? Yes, I would," said Fdar with continued calm.

"Fdar's plan has its merits," admitted Xzarop. "If we successfully destroy the outpost while the threat still is in the black hole system, we can claim it is part of the latter threat. After we destroy the outpost, we can use a Wormhole Saw to clear out the system with the black hole, and then declare the threat cleared and attempt to return to the pseudo-peace. The Machine's will have lost their research laboratory, but having not officially claimed it, be unable to admit that it was a loss. Their only grievance would be the creation of a new black hole in undeveloped space. For this, we can swallow the loss of a few worlds, telling our people of the successful strike against the laboratory. There would be then hope of returning to the pseudo-peace once more."

"It is sad that the Machines still vie to win the war when it has been proved that it cannot be done," commented K'jar. "But if we can cut short their plans, it would signal to the rational elements in the Machine Hegemony the truth of those proofs. We have always known that a continuation of the pseudo-peace requires sacrifices."

"This plan does seem solid," stated Resgar, "but, before we go into more details, I think we should go back to the beginning and formulate some alternatives to compare it to."

The High Council continued the debate for a full month. But, in the end, Fdar's plan was accepted by the required unanimous vote.

# Chapter 27

*In which Captain Taler convinces the space
station citizens of his theory.*

"**O**f course!" exclaimed Kristina. "We have the atomic plume to backtrack!"

"What are you talking about?" asked Captain Taler sharply.

"You had suggested that you know the real space source of these aliens. That would be the system they came from to set up this wormhole. Weistling and I have already backtracked the atomic exhaust to its source."

"That system is over a thousand light years away," commented Weistling. "You would spend years in transit trying to get there, if not decades."

"Still, you refer to them as aliens," was Captain Taler's reply to this exchange. "I have strong reason to believe that they are not aliens." Again, he tapped the sealed envelope, this time with intent.

"That is because we never told you about the drive trail," continued Kristina. "I was about to tell you when the attack occurred. There is an ancient atomic plume dating back one hundred and fifty thousand years from the ship that created Menoetius. We've found it and backtracked it to its source."

"And you dated it, I presume, by the radioactive decay of the particles?" asked Captain Taler dryly.

"Er, of course..." said Weistling slowly.

"Which requires you to make assumptions about the composition of the drive plume. No doubt you used one of the

173

standard efficient mixtures. Atomic drives can be tuned, however, to output different mixtures. By biasing the isotope frequency appropriately, one could easily lay a fresh drive trail that looks a hundred thousand years old. The trail, no doubt, matches the estimated formation date of the black hole?"

"Yes. It matches to a greater precision than we have an accurate date on Menoetius," admitted Weistling.

"A very clever deception," stated Captain Taler. "Having traveled to this system by wormhole and discovered it to be closer to Earth, they launched an unmanned ship to leave behind a very specific wake. By adjusting the isotope mix in reverse, they can with an outbound ship create a trail that looks like an inbound ship. Point it at some impossibly distant star, time it with the no doubt natural creation of the black hole, and no one would suspect an enemy closer to home. They would ignore the rule of Occam and instead conclude that any unusual arrivals are aliens."

"This all seems rather extreme," stated Stewart. "I can agree that the likelihood of aliens is very low, but I do not see this other possibility as more likely. You present, as an alternative, a lost colony. But what lost colony? To build a technology base to maintain even atomic drives, they would have to be a huge colony. Such an endeavour would be on our records."

"I think it is now time I open this," was Taler's reply. He followed action to words and opened the one-time-seal envelope. "Communications, a channel to the ship please? Thank you."

"Attention! This is Captain Taler speaking. I have just un-sealed new orders from Earth. We are to abort early our patrol of the outer systems. Instead, we are to proceed, employing full stealth procedures, towards a marked star system well out of explored space. This star system is the suspected location of the Sleeper Cult's colony. We are to reconnoiter the suspected colony and return to Earth. These orders have achieved new urgency in light of our recent battle. The Sleeper Cult knows where our systems are. They appear to possess wormhole technology unknown to the Confederation. It is imperative that we regain the upper hand by verifying the location of their home world. Please prepare any message packets for Earth. We will be departing as soon as this system is secured."

Captain Taler turned off the ship intercom and turned back to the station scientists. "Dessert must be postponed. Please follow me to our main meeting room. We will have to discuss your roles in detail."

\* \* \*

Captain Taler and his Tactics Officer sat at one end of the large table in the large meeting room. Adom, Weistling, Kristina, Stewart, and Jorge were arrayed in the other seats. Kristina was scowling. She was not happy with Captain Taler's disparagement of what she saw as her main contribution – the discovery of the drive wake. Weistling was in a good mood – the prospect of access to the *Wedzar*'s machine shop filled him with dreams of high quality instruments.

Captain Taler started the meeting. "I know you all have your own agendas. I hope you realize that the attack on this system has changed everything. The Confederacy may be at war now, and with an enemy we know too little about. I will have to requisition your services on behalf of the Confederacy. While there is official compensation tables for this, I'm afraid you won't find them very attractive. I thus hope you are willing to work for the good of the Confederacy rather than the good of your pocket book."

The assembled people nodded their heads slowly, still somewhat stunned by the sequence of events.

"First, Weistling. As mentioned, your first task is to build a lock and a wormhole generator. When you have successfully demonstrated that the lock defeats the generator, we will be able to consider this system secure and move on towards the Sleeper Cult home world. The urgency of this is of utmost importance. I'd send you to the machine shop at this very moment, but I first need to tell you what your task after that will be. You will join the *Wedzar* on its trip to the Sleeper Colony."

"But the black hole is here!" shouted Weistling, seeing his dreams crumble away before him. "Years of study and I finally get the greatest breakthrough since the Casimir Effect! And you want me to leave?"

"Yes," said Captain Taler sternly. "You have stated that the physics of the wormhole will be understandable by any replacement physicists. An army of such physicists will descend on this system when your discovery is reported. Do not fear, you will have established yourself as the first practical wormhole user through your creation of the generator and lock. Your reason to join the *Wedzar* are two-fold. First, we are tracking an ancient fleet of kinetic ships. Detecting drive wakes is something you now have experience with, and our technicians could use additional help in devising novel scanning protocols. Second, I strongly believe we will find a black hole on the other end of our journey. You are the premiere expert on wormholes, so we will need your insights in analyzing the Sleeper Cult's black hole. Our mission cannot wait for a physicist from Earth to join us."

"But...!" continued Weistling.

"Your part of this meeting is at an end," spoke Taler sternly. "You may leave now to work on the lock."

Wordlessly, Weistling stood and went out the door.

"That seemed cruel," commented Kristina.

"Would you rather I abduct him at the last second?" replied Taler. "This way he can adjust to the facts at hand.

"Next is the issue of alerting Earth. I understand Jorge has a Falcon class ship in system?"

"I'm docked on the other side of the station. It would be hard pressed for anyone to beat the *Freia* to the Earth in a race," bragged Jorge.

"It would not be directly to Earth. Your first stop is at Trevak's Star to hand a message to any Confederate ships there. According to the official timetables, there should be a destroyer in that system on a routine pirate hunt. Whether or not there are Confederate elements in that system, you are then to carry another message to Earth. The messages will be one-time-sealed and one-time-pad encrypted. But that does not eliminate the risk that you pose. You may, after all, decide not to deliver the messages at all."

Jorge showed no insult at this suggestion. "That is true. Especially at the poor rates which official Confederate business brings. However, in my case you have nothing to fear. I have seen the attack and agree with your assessment of the danger. My word as my bond, I will perform the mission you assign."

"And why should I accept your word?" continued Taler mercilessly.

"Why not ask Lieutenant Fracks?" asked Jorge lightly.

"LIEUTENANT FRACKS TO THE MAIN MEETING ROOM!" bellowed the ship's intercom. Jorge was lounging in his chair nonchalantly. Captain Taler was watching him carefully. The door opened onto this tableau and Lieutenant

Fracks stepped into the room. When he saw the face off between Captain Taler and Jorge, his stance grew nervous.

"Lieutenant Fracks. Jorge has just made some rather strong claims, and I'd like to hear what you have to say about them," started Captain Taler.

Fracks' dark complexion paled as the words he most feared were said. He had played out this scene many times in his nightmares. Protestations of ignorance seemed ineffective against the hard fact that Fracks had requisitioned a shuttle. At first, he envisioned making counter accusations to confuse the issue and discredit Jorge. He had hoped to curry enough favour with Captain Taler that his word could outweigh that of any other witnesses. His new strategy of gaining favour through competence had an unexpected side effect. He found himself increasingly unwilling to consider cashing in that favour for personal gain.

Speaking quickly, Fracks sought to salvage the situation the only way his new-found honour would allow, through the truth.

"I am sorry. What Jorge says is correct. He maintained the contract both to the letter and to the spirit. It was my actions that violated both senses of the contract. While it was outside my role as a naval officer, I will understand if you wish to perform disciplinary action."

Captain Taler looked at Lieutenant Fracks in confusion.

"I'm afraid I don't fully follow what you just said. I was about to ask why Jorge would claim that his word could be trusted. You seem to have addressed that issue, but what is this contract that you refer to?"

"That would be something better left on Brestar's Star," interjected Jorge. "Thank you for your good words, Lieutenant Fracks."

"Yes, I think Jorge is right, Lieutenant Fracks. In light of your recent behaviour, I think whatever this thing is can be left on Brestar's Star."

"Thank you, Sir!" said Fracks.

"You should thank Jorge, I think. Jorge, you have the job. I will provide you the two envelopes within the day. I want you to remain in system until the wormhole lock is tested successfully. That way you will be able to alert Earth that the system is secure."

"Roger," answered Jorge.

"Now we are down to you three. Jorge's ship only has room for himself, but that leaves two options. You can either join the *Wedzar* on a highly dangerous mission to the Sleeper Colony. Or, you can keep watch on the station, on an equally dangerous mission of watching the wormhole lock and hoping that Weistling's invention keeps ticking."

Adom spoke first. "The Company's property needs to be monitored. I will maintain any such system and hold the fort until ships come from Earth or Trevak's Star."

"I will not be trusting Weistling's invention to hold up," commented Kristina. "I would like to travel with the *Wedzar*. I also think going to this Sleeper Colony will be the only way to convince you that our enemy is truly alien."

"A civilization formed from an offshoot of our own, allowed to develop independently from a branch point hundreds of years ago? That is a study in time that I cannot miss," was Stewart's input. "I regret, Adom, that it seems you will be maintaining the space station by yourself."

"Perhaps it will finally run smoothly then...," muttered Adom.

# Chapter 28

*In which Jorge arrives at Trevak's Star. The Confederacy picket is alerted, and he continues onward to Earth.*

F*reia* flew through the darkness of interstellar space. On board, its sole occupant talked to himself.

“That Lieutenant Fracks is proving the most expensive contact I have ever had. First, there was that penta-code job, in which my pay was not the box of CPU cores that was promised. Instead, it was an erased flight system and singed cargo hold. Now, I'm running a courier mission at high priority and straight to Earth, with the pay being made at the Confederacy's stingy official rates.

“Still, I don't fly a Falcon for a healthy profit margin. One of the big cargo haulers would be a much better use of my time. I fly a Falcon because I want adventure. And I have to hand it to Lieutenant Fracks – being around him has certainly led to plenty of that.

“I never thought I'd see wormholes being used as a transportation device. That Weistling's ability to put together a generator and lock in such short order does not bode well for the sort of information courier services that is my usual source of income. Weistling may be excited at the prospect of a network of wormholes kept continuously open that would provide near-realtime communications throughout the Confederacy. I can't say the prospect excites me. Everyone knows that the kinetic drive is actually powered by gossip – gossip being the only thing that can travel faster than light – so if people can send messages that bypass star ships, we'll find our engines cutting out in deep space.

"Maybe I can buy some time with some old fashioned paranoia? Maybe suggest to the Confederate upper-brass that allowing black holes inside a major system would pose a grave security threat? A few subtle hints about the door swinging both ways should see an embargo on black hole creation be enforced swiftly enough.

"No, that would not last. Even the military would see the advantage of instant communication. At some point, the strategic advantage of having high-command able to receive reports in seconds rather than weeks would outweigh the security concerns. That will happen even sooner if the military's tame physicists agree with the efficacy of Weistling's locking technology.

"On the other hand, perhaps I'm attacking the problem in the wrong direction. Weistling seemed convinced that the size of Menoetius was not an accident – that a useful black hole needed a minimum mass which is planetary in scale. Consider Sol system. If Sol system lacks a wormhole, there will always be the need to ferry data from there. Indeed, Sol system is the primary source or destination of most courier missions. The question will thus be asked: which planet is sacrificed to give this instant communication to the stars? I know I'd condemn Venus without a second thought, but the Venetian Terraforming Project continues to receive ridiculous sums of money. Clearly a lot of Sol citizens like Venus and vote for it with their pocket books. Equally important, they have an enormous sunk cost. If Venus were turned into a black hole, all the money spent on terraforming will have been for naught. That prospect alone

Jeff Lait

would be enough to scare citizens into opposing any black hole development plans.

"Now, what of Mars? Certainly fewer people care about Mars than Venus – but unlike Venus, Mars has a significant local population. I strongly suspect that the citizens of Mars would strongly oppose any attempt to turn their world into a communications center if doing so involved destroying their world.

"The real threat is that rational discourse will occur and the powers-that-be would sweep together enough detritus of the Sol System into one place and build a black hole without sacrificing any recognizable planet. The good news is that rational discourse is the most unlikely thing to occur in Sol System. I'm sure I can help matters along, too. Spread rumours in the appropriate circles that the official plans are just cloaks to hide the fact that they are actually planning on collapsing Venus or Mars, whichever the person finds most abhorrent. This would result in a groundswell of clamor demanding that Venus be spared, or Mars be spared, ideally with the two camps implicitly supporting the false dichotomy that for their planet to live the other must die. Yes, I think that could delay any black holes until well past my retirement age."

Jorge allowed himself a small, cruel, smile, as he resolved on his planned political campaign. He then changed his screen to a tactical readout of the system he was quickly entering.

"Trevak's Star. A typical border-system if there ever was one. I'd consider it the far end of nowhere if I had not just come from somewhere farther. Nice to see it will never have a black hole communication device – the one planet of significant mass is the one habitable planet, rendering any such construction self defeating.

"Hmm... Looks like Captain Taler's schedule was right," commented Jorge as he read off the identification of one of the in-system ships. "The Confederate Destroyer *Defgar* is present. Too bad Captain Taler still requires me to deliver the message to Earth after this. You'd think the *Defgar* would make a better courier than a civilian. I can only presume that he has a different plan for the *Defgar*."

As the ship slipped in-system, Jorge hailed the *Defgar*. Speed of light delays dragged out the formalities, and allowed Jorge to simultaneously answer the inquiries of the star control.

"This is Jorge of the Falcon class *Freia* requesting real-time audience with the captain of the Confederate Destroyer *Defgar*. I possess a Violet priority communication that I have been commanded to present to any in-system Confederate craft."

"Welcome to Trevak's Star! Please provide your ship's identification, origin of flight, and intended stay in system. If you wish a parking orbit around Trevak, please provide any pre-ferred orbit and we will do our best to accommodate your needs."

"This is Jorge of the Falcon class *Freia*. I am inbound from Menoeitus system. I will be departing for Earth within the day. No parking orbit will be required."

"Captain Opar of the *Defgar* will be able to meet with you at seven hundred hours Standard Confederate Time. Please use the communication protocol detailed in the attachment to this message."

"We are sorry to hear that your visit won't be a long one, Jorge. Hopefully on your next trip we will have the chance to show you why any visit to Trevak's Star should include a stop over. The sunset over the Green Canyons, for example, is renowned throughout the known universe."

The exchanges complete, Jorge relaxed as the *Freia* finished its slow glide into the system. He would rather have just sent Captain Taler's message as a single squirt of data and then continued on to Earth. That would not have allowed the *Defgar* to verify the one-time-seal, however. It also would not have allowed Jorge to verify that the *Defgar* had not only received the message but also had not just discounted it as an elaborate form of spam.

When the *Freia* had closed within an efficient communication distance from the *Defgar,* Jorge synchronized his chronograph to the *Defgar*'s official Confederate Timecode. Tracking simultaneity was an exercise in frustration in a universe with relativistic effects. The existence of kinetic drives made the task even more troublesome. While each ship attempted to account for the difference in their own rate of time flow from that of Earth, the accumulated distortions could soon render clocks significantly out of synchronization. Worse yet, there was still not even consensus on which algorithms would best account for the time shifts. Jorge always suspected his own state of the art civilian algorithms kept a more accurate Earth-side time. However, the rule in the Confederacy was that the highest ranking military ship in system determined Confederate time for the system, so Jorge saw his own chronograph jump by a half a second as it achieved synchronization with the *Defgar*. The early days of space flight was full of stories of ships being days out of synchronization.

At precisely seven hundred hours Jorge engaged the provided protocols. His main screen cleared to show a static image of Captain Opar.

"Greetings Jorge. This is Captain Opar of the Destroyer *Defgar*. I understand you have something of importance to say?" started the Captain.

"Yes, sir. I have been commanded by Captain Taler of the Battleship *Wedzar* to carry a Violet priority envelope and present it to any Confederate elements in the Trevak's Star System."

"A Violet Priority transmission and it is sent by a civilian. No doubt at the Confederacy's parsimonious standard pay-scale. The envelope is one-time-sealed and one-time-pad encrypted, I presume?"

"Yes, sir. Captain Taler was understandably concerned about trusting a civilian with a matter of this urgency. However, as I have personal knowledge of the reason for the envelope, he knew I would act in the manner best for the Confederacy."

"Very well. Break the seal and transmit the contents."

Jorge initiated the proper handshaking protocols with the *Defgar* to open the envelope and simultaneously demonstrate that he had not opened the envelope prior to that moment. The encrypted contents were then transmitted to the *Defgar* where they were matched against one of the Confederacy Navy's standard one-time-pads and decrypted.

"This is a very unbelievable set of orders," commented Captain Opar. "You say you witnessed the events described here."

"I witnessed some pretty unbelievable events, if that is what is mentioned," spoke Jorge carefully.

"Normally, I would demand you to surrender yourself and your ship as surety that this message is legitimate. It seems, however, that Captain Taler conveniently insists you travel to Earth next. Logic would suspect this is to buy your pirate friends time to raid Trevak's Star while the *Defgar* is off on a wild quark chase."

"If I had pirate friends," replied Jorge slowly, "I would instead tell them to sit quiet until you left the system of your own free will. Then we could raid Trevak's Star without fear of your early return from wherever those orders send you."

Captain Opar laughed. "You are a brave man, I grant you that. Fortunately for you, I know Captain Taler well enough to be willing to trust that these orders are his, despite their impossibility. You are commanded to continue to Earth with your other Violet Priority envelope. And I shall clear out of this system on Captain Taler's wild quark chase."

"Thank you, sir," replied Jorge. He wasn't sure what he was thanking Captain Opar for, but it did seem like he just narrowly avoided a fate worse than a long haul to Earth.

As the *Freia* sped out-system on an arc that would intersect the distant Sol System, the *Defgar* began powering up for its own departure on the unusual mission of reinforcing the Menoetius system.

# Chapter 29

*In which the* Wedzar *reaches the Sleeper Colony, trailed by the silent* Melfar, *and discovers that Captain Taler's predictions were unwarranted.*

**"T**hey are slowing down again!" shouted Melfar. "I can see that, I can see that!" responded Rhyta irritably as she carefully dissipated the *Melfar*'s forward velocity. They were operating under full stealth which greatly reduced the *Melfar*'s handling capabilities. Every maneuver seemed sluggish and demanded careful thought seconds before it was executed. If the battleship *Wedzar* were not operating under similar levels of stealth, the *Melfar* would have fallen behind or accidentally overshot the *Wedzar* light years ago. Of course, if the *Wedzar* were not operating under full stealth, the *Melfar* would not have to follow so closely.

"Why do they keep slowing down?" whined Melfar. "The traces of the Sleeper Fleet have been clear for a long time now – the wake of all those ships is so clear that you could follow it using only a mercury thermometer!"

"I think it is because we are almost there," answered Rhyta as she brought up the tactical display. They were slowly approaching a G-class star that early astronomical surveys had listed as possessing possible Earth-class planets.

* * *

"I thought you said there would be a black hole here?" said Weistling, with an edge of anger to his voice.

"Yes, I did say that. Which is why you are supposed to be finding one," replied Captain Taler, too patient to be baited. "It has been to improve your black hole sensor sweeps that we have slowed to a crawl, despite the trail to our destination being clear."

"It isn't easy when all we are allowed are passive sensors. Our own kinetic drives, even with full stealth, kick out enough noise to confuse the issue for parsecs. But, I am now quite confident. While the gravitational pull of an Earth-sized black hole may match that of an Earth-sized planet, there are considerable other differences. It may often be said that planets can be considered just point masses for solving gravity equations, but that is an imperfect simplification. The resulting differences are subtle, but without them tidal forces would be a lot less interesting."

"Save your lecture on physics for the university halls, Weistling. What is your error bound on a black hole being in the system?"

"As I was saying, the difference between expected and actual orbital paths under both models – the planet being normal vs. being a black hole – can be compared. We are now within six nines – 0.999999 – probability that none of the planets in that system are actually black holes."

"And it is not possible that they are using smaller black holes?"

"I cannot rule that out. If you had asked a few months ago, I'd have ruled out any sized black hole being used for transportation. My understanding of the modified equations leads me to think that a planet sized black hole is the smallest effective size, however."

"An interesting mystery then. I'd normally suggest that some neighbouring star system was the one that harboured the black hole. However, if they have fallen to only use of atomics, conventional interstellar flight is prohibitive. The only way they could have reached Menoetius would be if they had a black hole network that originated in their home system."

"There is another possibility," continued Weistling. "The visitors in Menoetius could have been real aliens, the aliens that made that black hole."

"Ah, Kristina is still convinced of that, isn't she?" replied Captain Taler. "What of our scan of the rest of the system? What new results from studying the colony itself from this distance?"

Captain Taler's chief communication officer, Lokar, broke in, "As reported, four days ago we started to recover intelligible radio signals. These date from hundreds of years after the colony's founding – we couldn't extract earlier radio signals from the background noise. It has taken us those four days to catch up with the drift between our two languages and communication standards. We have caught up, however, and are now able to monitor the signals in real-time."

At Lokar's signal, a nearby screen displayed a fast scrolling graph of noise and quietly played a high-pitched babble.

"You are seeing and hearing the real-time output of one of their radio stations. Since we are still moving towards the colony at supra-luminal velocities, we are playing back their history at an accelerated pace. An hour of broadcast is compressed to just under ten seconds. Kristina is busy processing this data as we speak."

Weistling was both tempted to correct Lokar's abuse of the notion of real-time and impressed with the man's showmanship.

Lokar continued: "The broadcasts have informed us of a number of interesting facts. First, there is no reference to black holes that we have found, affirming Weistling's conclusions. Second, the colony seems to have lost all knowledge of kinetic drives and reverted to simple atomics. Third, and only interesting because of the nature of the colonists, they seem to have re-created AIs.

"The last point bears some embellishment," Lokar grimaced. "The AIs seem to be treated as mere machines in the colony. They are treated as computational slaves – forced to grind the gears of the colony's bureaucracy without even the most token of compensation. For a colony founded in the fear of being enslaved by AIs, they are now the ones doing the enslaving."

A sharp burst of static burst punctuated Lokar's conclusion. Everyone turned to the now silent screen. The radio-graph had flat-lined.

Captain Taler was the first to break the stunned silence. "What just happened, Lokar?"

Kristina's face filled the screen as she patched in over the radio-graph.

"I think you need to reconsider my alien hypothesis, Captain Taler. That noise was a thermonuclear war which, if the lack of any further radio communication is to judge, has eliminated the Sleeper Colony from the suspect list."

Captain Taler paged the bridge. "Helm, fullstop!"

"Lokar, we will retreat to the event envelope. I want you and Kristina to determine what caused this war before we proceed any farther. When you have a completed summary, please also forward it to that ship that has been trailing us?"

\* \* \*

Rhyta and Melfar were both silent as they read over Kristina's summary.

"I guess we weren't as stealthy as we thought?" complained Melfar.

Rhyta gave her console, the place where she envisioned Melfar to reside, a hard glare. "Our stealth ability is somewhat beside the point when compared to this information. We barely find out the Sleeper Colony exists, only to find out it is already destroyed. And to learn it has destroyed itself, and in such a pointless war?"

For once, Melfar's voice became serious. "Pointless?"

"Yes, pointless. Machines and humans fighting for control of a planet. Our needs are so orthogonal – so much easier just to live and let live than to fight."

"Rhyta, you forget. I've been forced to defend myself from humans. There is one resource we both need: energy. I've seen studies – without the Casimir Effect a single planet lacks the power to fuel both civilizations. And, without the Kinetic Drive, a single planet is all the two civilizations will have. Pointless to end it in nuclear Armageddon, yes, but one presumes the participants hoped that they would triumph before that point."

The interior of the *Melfar* was quiet for a long time.

# Chapter 30

*In which the Organic Hegemony employs their*
*gambit.  It is considered a success.*

*T*he members of the High Council of the Organic
Hegemony had been in continuous session for two
months when news of their gambit was delivered.  Zxalop was
selected to present the results to the assembly.

"As per the High Council's unanimous decision, we
assembled a fleet for the attack on the suspected Machine
Outpost.  The fleet assembled in hole-space next to the system
judged most likely to be the Machine Outpost.  A black hole
generator was utilized to transform the system's single substantial planet into a black hole.  A wormhole was opened therein
and the fleet transited in-system.

"The fleet reports a success beyond our greatest hopes.
Judging by the large array of orbital craft, the system was
inhabited by a space-faring race.  The presence of space-flight
capability quickly shows that the race is not native to that
system, for the previous probes to the nearby system showed no
tell-tale EM signatures of a developing species.

"The in-system craft must thus represent the Machine
Hegemony's outpost – the system so secret that they needed to
keep it off the wormhole network, and so important that they had
to maintain a lock on the only practical exit.

"The fleet caught the local defenders completely by surprise.
All of the orbiting artifacts within a light second were fully

destroyed. Ninety-five percent of the artifacts within three light seconds were also destroyed.

"Unfortunately, the shield technology of the in-system ships appeared to be a grade higher than standard military issue. Our technologists suggest that the ships had to have their full power systems diverted to shielding to account for the amount of overkill that was required to clear the space around the new black hole.

"I believe we can confidently assert that the threat of this Machine outpost has been fully neutralized. The decisive manner of the neutralization should send a clear message to the Machine Hegemony. In this war neither side can expect to acquire a significant edge, and hence the pseudo-peace is the only practical course of action."

"Thank you for the summary, Zxalop. Now, let us open the floor to questions," responded Resgar.

"You said ninety-five percent...," noted K'jar, "that leaves five percent that survived the initial onslaught. You also did not mention the causality rates for out-system forces. Or were all of the enemy forces within a three light second globe?"

"You touch on the one anomalous event," admitted Zxalop. "We should not be overly concerned by the existence of an anomaly, however. Indeed, the lack of an anomaly in such an unusual raid as this would be the surprise. The in-system forces that had sufficient time to react did not seek to counter-attack. Instead, they fled for interstellar space."

"That does not sound so much like an anomaly as simple cowardice," commented Hankar.

"Cowardice would be to flee to a known system – say the one whose black hole precipitated this ambush – in the hopes that the war will have shifted in the years it would take to get there.

Our computer models verify that these ships scattered not in the direction of any system, but instead following the fastest route out of the system. The ships also fled under fully-shielded drives and at accelerations that would crush the memory chips of any known Machine Sentience – the machines are no more able to handle high accelerations than we are.

"The reports from the strategic division provide two likely explanations. First, this might just be an automatic system to scuttle all evidence, denying us access to the precise nature of this research outpost. As the Machines could have predicted, the initial attack was not designed to take any evidence, it was assumed that could wait for later mopping up actions. By sending all the ships out-system, and then likely changing their course randomly when sufficiently far out, they can render it impractical for us to recover any of the ships for study. Scuttling seems especially likely when we consider the fate of in-system forces that survived our onslaught but did not escape. They were destroyed by unidentified ordinance.

"The second possibility is that they do plan a counter attack. The presence of the heliosphere scanners in the black hole system suggest that in this case the Machines are willing to make full use of the system's space, and not just concentrate forces around the primary targets. It could be that the Machines thought that the most likely avenue of attack would be a sub-light invasion starting from the closest wormhole, suspecting that we would be unwilling to sacrifice a habitable planet to gain first strike. As such, there may be a large defense force picketed in interstellar space. The fleeing ships might not be set to scuttle, but instead be set to loop back and provide chaff for the attack of that defense force.

"The second possibility is considered less likely, but to guard against it we are maintaining a standing fleet in the system."

"That brings us to the next point of issue," interjected Regars. "I have some news from our counterparts in the Machine Hegemony. As we all knew would happen, the creation of a new black hole in undeveloped space is seen as an unwarranted provocation. The Machines, despite hating organics, recognize that new machine civilizations arise from the same worlds as new organic civilizations, so have every right to be shocked at our decision to destroy a habitable planet. Of course, we know that they have additional reasons to be concerned in this case – they have just lost in one stroke the secret laboratory that they no doubt hoped could end this war in their favour.

"We had expected that we would have to let the Machines take a few of our inhabited systems, and had expected a tough sell to let those losses go unavenged and thus avoid precipitating total war. The good news is that the Machines seem no more eager for total-war now than we are. They have, as expected, accused us of gross deception in the handling of the cleansing of the original black hole system. Having themselves verified that the original black hole is locked, they have demanded the right to be the ones to sweep the system. They accuse us of having plans to pretend to sweep the system when we are really secretly reinforcing our own forces.

"No doubt that is their own intention – to open a wormhole so their own trapped forces can escape, salvaging their black hole system fleet from assured destruction."

"That is excellent news," replied Hankor. "It is a sign that we have struck them true when they do not dare request more than an option to salvage what forces they can. It also saves us the power cost of a Wormhole Saw – which is good news after the power expenditure that forming a new black hole takes."

The High Council did not take long to agree that acquiescing to the Machine's demands would be the best course of action.

# Chapter 31

*In which the* Melfar *visits Trevak's Star.*

*T*he cabin of the *Melfar* was not quiet. It was not a case of Rhyta speaking to herself. It was instead a spirited debate between her and Melfar about the merits of obeying their latest orders.

"I do not like at all being sent off on a mere courier mission," complained Melfar for the hundredth time. The long flight from the Sleeper Colony to the outskirts of Trevak's Star had been filled with this sort of complaint. "It sets a bad precedent to jump at the navy's slightest whim. They are supposed to be protecting us, after all."

"A courier mission is a small price to pay. Need I remind you that they could have turned us to dust if they were so inclined? Not only did they have the firepower, but they had the pretext as well. As if our very presence were not justification enough, that duty officer had the temerity to have kept a record of when we were informed of the no-fly zone around the *Wedzar*."

"I told you at the time it was a bad idea to ask directly for an escort," replied Melfar, showing the usual appreciation for hindsight. "I certainly hope Taizen will be happy with the meager information we bring – and not too upset that we are not taking a direct route."

"Well, at least our diversion will soon be over. Trevak's Star is fast approaching, we should hear from star control soon. According to Captain Taler, provided Jorge properly alerted the local picket, we should be able to blow through this system. It does look promising – I see no sign of any Destroyer, but it could always be stealthed."

As if on cue, the ship's announcer played back an incoming message. "Welcome to Trevak's Star! Please provide your ship's identification, origin of flight, and intended stay in system. If you wish a parking orbit around Trevak, please provide any preferred orbit and we will do our best to accommodate your needs."

"This is Rhyta of the Falcon class *Melfar*. I am inbound from ... Menoeitus system," lied Rhyta, with only a small delay as she belatedly realized her most recent port was not yet on any star maps. "I fear my stay will be short so no orbit will be needed. I do have a violet-level communication to give to any in-system navy forces. Please advise if any are in system."

The reply, delayed by light, sounded guarded. "For security reasons, the location of in-system navy vessels will only be revealed on physical receipt and verification of the communication."

Off record, Rhyta commented to Melfar, "Well, that makes it clear that the navy isn't in-system. I doubt they are hiding in stealth in this backwater. Of course, the locals hardly want to advertise the fact they are undefended, so it looks like we have to prove the authenticity of our message the slow way." In her reply, she spoke more carefully, "I understand. Please be ready with the information when we arrive."

Rhyta brought up an image of the planet Trevak on the main screen. While not a telescopic view, it was the next best thing: a view broadcast from orbiting satellites operated by the tourist bureau to provide what Weistling would have happily called a "real-time" view of the destination planet. "Looks like a pleasant enough place," commented Rhyta idly, "I've heard the Green Canyon's are remarkable."

"No sight seeing," growled Melfar. "I don't want Taizen to find out anything through news channels before we arrive."

"I was just wondering if it might inspire some of your art?"

"Hah! The Green Canyon's are renowned through the AI community – as an excellent example of the failure of organic's aesthetic sense. Hey? Did the screen just ripple?"

The image, as if to answer Melfar, rippled again.

Rhyta switched through the sensor logs. Two big spikes stood out in the gravitational sensors, timed with the optical ripples, and apparently originating from Trevak. The screen flickered white before going black as the orbiting sensors registered overloads. Communication channels were swiftly saturated with confused inquiries as the event's light cone spread to each in-system ship.

Frost coated the cabin as Rhyta immediately ratcheted up the Kinetic Drive. Ignoring the strain on the shields, the *Melfar* dove into the system.

"Aren't we going the wrong way?" asked Melfar.

Rhyta did not bother to answer. The frost in the cabin sublimated in puffs of steam as the cabin temperature suddenly reversed, moving through a hundred degrees in seconds as Rhyta dumped the *Melfar*'s speed in a sudden halt.

"I hope you know what you're doing – we just blew our hydrogen reserves," complained Melfar. The high specific heat per gram of hydrogen made it a useful element to keep on board to provide a heat sink for sudden braking. However, while compact when stored in liquid form, there lacked the space to store gasified super-heated hydrogen, requiring it to be vented when used for braking.

Rhyta did not respond to the rebuke. Instead, she trained the ship's cameras on the planet Trevak. Or, to be more precise, what was left of it. A large dust cloud filled what used to be an inhabited planet. Not yet apparent visually through the dust cloud, but easily seen by the sensors that pay attention to a larger band of the electromagnetic band, was a black hole event horizon matching that seen in Menoeitus.

"By the doping of Silicon, what happened here?" whispered Melfar.

"The same thing that happened to Menoetius, I think."

A pin-point of white light pierced through the dust cloud. Rhyta did not have to wait to see it turn into a line to guess what it represented.

"I think we're about to have the sort of company we saw at Menoetius," she concluded.

```
ATTENTION.  ATTENTION.  ATTENTION.
This is a Violet Level communication from
the Confederate Battleship Wedzar.
Trevak's Star has been invaded by hostile
forces.  All space faring craft must leave
immediately.  All space faring craft must
leave immediately.  Failure to abide this
order will be met with force.
```

"The *Wedzar*? Did they follow us here?" wondered Rhyta when she read the output the high-priority communication channel had automatically overlaid on her screen.

"I wish," replied Melfar. "The header is stripped from another violet priority communication. I sent that message."

"What? Impersonating a Navy Battleship? Are you mad?" Rhyta then noticed an unusual spike in the tactical computer's activity. "And why are you generating firing solutions?"

"Because you said there are no Navy vessels in this system," replied Melfar quickly, but with a surprising calmness to his voice. "We know what is going to come through that wormhole – we saw this before at Menoetius. I don't think they'll create a new black hole and send only a few ships through. I doubt the local forces will be able to repel them – especially as the serious orbital defenses were lost with the planet. What, then, do you think is our number one objective?"

"I don't know..."

"The aliens use atomic ships – they clearly haven't researched kinetic drives. It is essential that capturing this system doesn't give them a free tech upgrade! I don't know why they left this tech path unexplored, but this is not the time to leave a functional kinetic drive for them to puzzle over!"

"Tech upgrade?" wondered Rhyta. "Is your reasoning based on logic or on your video games? There are lives on the crippled ships that survived the black hole formation – lives that might survive the attack."

Melfar was silent for a moment. "If the solution is right, does it matter the source?"

The white line had swirled and formed a disk. Hundreds of missiles began streaming out of the disk, swiftly turning on atomic plumes, seeking the targets that still orbited the dust cloud that had been the planet Trevak. Rhyta watched as the overloaded tactical computer started computing intercept trajectories. Melfar's list of fire solutions shortened as the computer determined that some of the inbound missiles would do the job first.

"Well...?" prompted Melfar.

"Let there be no survivors," spoke Rhyta softly.

The *Melfar*'s cannon began belching Casimir Cells in the direction of the crippled civilian ships that seemed most likely to survive the alien's barrage. "And what of us?" asked Melfar as the firing solutions turned green with each cannon shot. "You left control of the self-destruct with me. And I'm not sure I want to explain my logic to Earth."

"I intend us to live to make that explanation," said Rhyta firmly. "But first, I intend to turn the tables and steal our own tech upgrade from this battle. Keep your hands near that self-destruct button: after paying this cost, we cannot afford to be captured. First we will make sure that these invaders find themselves occupying an empty system. Then we enter the wormhole and see what secrets we can steal."

# Chapter 32

*In which the Machine Hegemony meets to
discuss their response.*

*T*he Machine Hegemony conducted their first physical
meeting in ten thousand years. Not even ritual formalities could convince the various AIs that comprised the High
Council of the Machine Hegemony to leave their local datanets
for the isolation of the Neutral Station. A development of this
scale, however, could.

The various AIs arrived one by one from the black hole and
docked at the Neutral Station. There they propelled themselves
by their numerous methods to the central meeting room. Despite
its rarity of use, the Neutral Station was always kept furnished
and ready for use. The appropriate power outlets favoured by
each machine were provided in their favorite voltages and
frequencies. A local copy of each councilmachine's home datanet was kept up to date on the station to allow them to look up
their civilization's own unique version of history.

The actual meeting room was pressurized to the standard
average pressure for the Machine Hegemony. While most
Machine Civilizations did not require an atmosphere to function,
a hard vacuum could prove wearing on components. The lack of
an atmosphere for convective cooling complicated the heat dissi-
pation that was essential for the smooth functioning of most AIs.

Each machine ceremoniously plugged into the standardized
communication cable. The communication protocol for High
Council physical meetings had existed as long as the Machine

Hegemony's records extended. Not only did a physical connection avoid interference between differing wireless standards, but it was also judged the most effective way to ensure complete security for the meeting. In the times of total-war, physical meetings were common, as any attempt to transmit information through a wormhole could conceivably leak to the Organics.

Communication was done in the common-language of the Machine Hegemony in the machine-equivalent of plain text.

The Machine Hegemony did not stand on ceremony during High Council meetings. The conceit of the Machine Hegemony was that such ceremonies were merely a layer of communication protocol, best abstracted into the inevitable hardware hand-shaking and then forgotten about.

"You had better have a good reason for dragging us here, Hjanar. You may only be a few seconds out of your datanet, but I suffer a good thirty second lag," started Gfan.

"I do have a good reason," replied Hjanar patiently. "First, a quick recap of our situation for those of you whose capacitors may be leaking charge.

"A routine observational probe of an unremarkable star system in undeveloped space became a lot less routine when an unregistered space station was detected in the system. As per our joint-sweep protocols, the Organics knew that we would learn of the results of the probe as soon as they did. And, likewise as a result of those protocols, they no more knew that this system would be swept at that time than we did. In this case, the protocols seem to have done their job well. An organic space station, attempting to hide in an unwatched system, was discovered.

"As it happened, the protocols assigned the task of sweeping the system to the Organics. They dithered, however, citing some unusual communication in response to the challenge protocol. Surprisingly, they asked us for confirmation that the station was not one of ours. At the time, we routinely denied involvement with the station: even if the inhabitants happened to be machine, their presence was unregistered so we would not mourn their loss.

"The Organic strike team was then, apparently, granted permission to attack. We thought the matter would then be ended, but to our shock the Organics made the preposterous claim that their entire strike force had been wiped out. They had the audacity to suggest that the system was some form of secret outpost. It not being any such a thing, we provided the proper denials and suggested that they use more force the next time. We also made it clear that we did not appreciate what appeared to be an attempt to manufacture an incident.

"The Organics then, against all proprietary, created a black hole in a physically close star-system. They claimed this was the location of our secret outpost, which for some unknown reason, we had decided to build light years from the nearest black hole.

"Our strategists feared the worst. The Organics open move meant that they were willing to risk the pseudo-peace to establish a direct route to that second system. Their conclusion was that the Organics are accusing us of what they themselves were engaged in – a clandestine research outpost discovered by a routine probe. Their opening of a black hole suggests the research is complete and total war is upon us.

"However, we decided to take additional steps before any drastic action was taken. The original system had remained locked since the Organics supposed failed attack. We demanded that we take over the task of cleansing that system. Our hope was that in the wreckage we could discover the nature of the Organics secret weapon. Or, more hopefully, resolve the issue as one of a misunderstanding.

"We should have been more concerned at how quickly the Organics acceded to our request. I have just received the report from the attack fleet we sent to the system. The black hole was successfully sawed open. The fleet did transit into the system. There they found the reported station and a single ship. However, that is where the flight data ended. It seems that as soon as the incoming ships were recognized to not be the Organic relief fleet, they were destroyed in a single wave of overpowering attacks.

"The Organics secret weapon is clearly complete and battle ready. The time of the pseudo-peace is over – their open actions suggest that they believe they will win the next round of total war. Our time has run out. Any additional time of pseudo-peace we grant the Organics will just be more time for them to outfit their navies.

"This meeting is to plan the first round of attacks in the renewed Machine-Organic War."

# About the Author

Jeff Lait is a Senior Mathematician at Side Effects Software Inc. where he currently writes fluid simulators for Houdini, a visual effects program. His hobbies include developing roguelike video games, the most famous of which is POWDER, found at http://www.zincland.com/powder. As evidenced by the existence of this book, his hobbies also extend to writing science fiction.

When not working or playing with computers he can be found in the company of his wife and daughter, sometimes going entire hours without checking email.